THE
LOWER
CANYONS

JOHN MANUEL

atmosphere press

THE
LOWER
CANYONS

Also by JOHN MANUEL

The Natural Traveler Along North Carolina's Coast

The Canoeist

Hope Valley

For Burt Kornegay,
who introduced me to the Lower Canyons.

|One|

As his raft approached Woodall Shoals on the Chattooga River, Robbie Ducharme came erect in the stern. The rapid looked innocent enough from above, a sloping ledge that fed into a hissing sea of sunlit bubbles. But instead of drifting downstream, the bubbles ran upstream towards the base of the rapid, to a backward spinning wave called a "hydraulic." He knew that hydraulics came in all strengths, depending upon the river flow, some only powerful enough to hold in a can, others to trap a tree trunk. After an all night rain, the river high and muddy, Woodall was looking super grabby. Anyone who fell in here would be "Maytagged"—spun in circles. It would take an angel with a rope to pull you out.

Today, High Five Adventure's clients were 24 members of a Baptist church from Atlanta. Raft guides liked church groups. They followed orders and tended to tip well. At 34, Ducharme was the company's oldest guide, but because of his playful nature, he'd been given the youngest members—five girls in their early teens.

"Alright, ladies," he said as they approached the rapid. "All forward!"

The girls dug their paddles into the water. Or rather placed them in the water. In ten years of guiding, this had to be one of the weakest crews he'd known, particularly little pig-tailed Maria who sat with him in the back, gingerly holding her paddle above the surface.

"Come on, Maria, let's see some of that muscle. Stroke! Stroke! Stroke!"

As the raft slid over the edge and into the apron of bubbles, it stalled. The girls were not strong enough to free it from the backward pull, but with his long, sinewy arms, Ducharme pulled the raft out of trouble and on its way. Just another day on the job.

Below Woodall, the Chattooga slowed and widened, giving view to the clearing sky and the wooded ridgeline above the river. With the coming of warm weather, the hills were flush with color. Pinkish-green alder bushes lined the river's edge. Dogwood blossoms shone in the understory. Midway up, the oak trees posed in their sage green robes and tulip poplar waved their hands.

Nothing could top the Southern Appalachians in spring. Only the hemlocks were bare, every one killed by an invasive pest known as the wooly adelgid. The centuries-old giants looked like fire-bombed church steeples rising above a city of green. Now, scientists said, other trees were under attack—ash from the Emerald borer, laurels from the Ambrosia beetle, beech and dogwood from some kind of fungus. Nothing was safe from foreign invaders and a fast-changing climate.

As he steered the raft downriver, he chatted up his girls.

"Are any of you experienced paddlers or are you all newbies?" he said.

"I've been down the Chattahoochee," Jessica said. "We tipped over twice!"

"In a raft?"

"No, it was, like, a canoe."

"We'll try not to let that happen today," he said.

Maria frowned. "You mean we might tip over?"

"It's always a possibility. And what do we do if that happens?"

"Hold onto the raft," LaToya said.

"That's right. And what if we're too far away from the raft?"

"Swim to shore or look for someone to throw us a rope," said Jessica.

"Awesome. Give me a high five."

The crew raised their paddles and clapped them together in the rafting version of slapping hands.

Through the winding channel, the line of boats moved like a jointed snake. High Five always had a kayaker paddle out in front of the rafts to check for fallen trees and log jams, and another kayaker in back to pick up any swimmers. The six-person rafts were buoyant enough to get through almost any rapid, but they were slow to get started and hard to turn around.

Annie, the lead guide and a former collegiate swimmer, paddled the first raft. She was admired by the male guides for her physical strength and force of personality. None of them had trouble taking orders from her. Toby, nicknamed Ickabod for his pale skin and long, bony frame paddled second. He and Ducharme competed for the best facial hair, the former sporting a blonde Fu Manchu moustache with corkscrew tips, and he a big, black beard that hung like a spade from his face. Temo, the strongest guide and Ducharme's closest friend, paddled the third raft.

5

As the boats drifted through the slow water, Ducharme saw an opportunity for a little mischief.

"Y'all ready for some fun?" he said to his crew. "We're going to execute a sneak attack on Temo's raft."

He paddled silently forward and, at a distance of ten feet, gave the order. "Attack! Attack!" The girls slapped their paddles across the surface and sent a shower of cold water onto Temo's head. The big guide spun around and prepared to retaliate.

"All back," Ducharme shouted.

As Ducharme's raft pulled out of range, Temo pointed. "You're going to get it, Ducharme. Just when you least expect it."

Annie turned around to see the cause of the commotion. She waited until the other rafts came abreast of hers.

"Y'all having fun?" she said to his crew. "Is Robbie filling you with stories?"

"He said he lost his finger in a sword fight," LaToya said, referring to Ducharme's missing pinkie.

"Yeah, right," Temo said. "He cut it off himself."

That was true. He'd lost it in a high school shop class while distractedly feeding a board into a band saw.

"Do you know how to tell when a raft guide is lying?" Annie said.

The girls shook their heads.

"His lips are moving."

Some of the kids laughed. Others seemed confused. He guessed sarcasm wasn't in the Baptist's nomenclature.

"Alright, from here on down, it's all big rapids," Annie said. "We've got five Class IV's and two Class V's."

Class IV rapids were tough, with big waves or tight

passages that required complex maneuvering. Ducharme had run enough Class IV's that he wasn't afraid of them. Class V rapids had the same badass features, plus being located in a part of the river that made it difficult to rescue anyone who fell overboard. And if you flipped your raft in a Class V? Forget it.

"Guides, give each other space," Annie said. "I want plenty of room in case we have to rescue a swimmer."

The guides tapped the top of their helmets, the universal sign for "Understood."

They set their rafts in motion. The gorge narrowed, steep slopes becoming cliffs. Giant slabs of rock, fallen from above, littered the banks. Some lay in the channel, dividing it into blind alleys. Others lodged at bends in the river and were undercut by the swift current. You did not want to get sucked into an undercut rock.

As Ducharme rounded a bend, a sound like a train crossing a bridge arose in the distance. He knew that every instinct was telling his crew to be afraid, to back away.

"Seven Foot Falls!" he yelled. "All forward!"

One by one, the rafts ahead disappeared over the ledge. With two powerful draws, he lined his up for the rapid. The bow pitched downward, a jumble of rock and whitewater thrown into view. The raft rode the narrow flume and slammed into the downstream wave. Jessica, in the front seat, pitched over the side. She bobbed to the surface, eyes wide with terror.

He yelled, "Grab the raft!"

Some of the girls reached out to their tripmate. The current slowed. In one swift motion, he stowed his paddle, grabbed Jessica's lifejacket by the shoulder straps and hauled her onboard.

"You O.K.?" he said.

Jessica nodded, short of breath.

"O.K. Get back in your seat." Another satisfied customer.

Next up was Crack in the Rock, named for the vein of rock that ran bank to bank, save for three narrow openings. Two of these cracks were less than a yard wide and would trap any boat or swimmer that blundered into them. Approaching the Crack always gave Ducharme the creeps. A few years before, a young girl wading along the shore had slipped off a rock and been swept into the first crack. Despite the heroic effort of rescue crews, her body was pinned underwater for more than a month and when it finally came out, it was little more than a skeleton.

The one opening wide enough for a raft was often choked with logs. If that was the case, the boaters would have to pull ashore and portage their rafts around the rapid. Andrew, one of the two kayakers, paddled ahead to check for debris.

"It's open!" he yelled.

Ducharme held his position at the back of the line, waiting, as protocol required, for Temo to clear the drop.

"Here we go," he yelled. "All forward."

The raft squeezed through the opening and down the flume into still water. Piece of cake.

Below Crack in the Rock, the group pulled over to shore for a lunch break. The guides brought out coolers and distributed sandwiches and drinks to their clients, then gathered in their own circle off to one side. Annie inquired of Ducharme how his girls were doing.

"They're cool," he said. "Not the strongest group I've had."

"Robbie lost one going over the falls," Temo said. "I saw him give her a little shove with his paddle."

"She was only under for a few minutes," he said. "I hauled her in before she turned blue."

This was his favorite part of the job, the camaraderie and jousting with the other guides. His family was here on the river—he had no other. He tried not to think of what he would do when he grew older. Most guides physically wore out by age 40, a mere six years away. Maybe he'd be promoted to the front office. There were worse futures to contemplate.

He turned to Chris, one of the two kayakers, to ask about his recent trip out West. "Dude, how was the Rio Grande?"

"Awesome. Didn't see another soul for five days."

"What, no raft trips every four hours?"

"No rafts at all. Saw some people in canoes."

"Man, I would love to do canoes. Let people paddle their own craft."

"How was the scenery?" Annie said.

"Blows this place away," Chris said. "On this stretch called the Lower Canyons, the walls are 1,500 feet high!"

Annie shook her head, stood and examined the river. There were two more big rapids left, Jawbone and Soc 'Em Dog, in close succession, and together they made a dangerous combination. Jawbone featured a twisting passage through a maze of boulders and over multiple drops, ending in a plunge through a "hole," a deep depression between two waves. This hole had a tendency to flip rafts, so High Five made sure both kayakers were positioned onshore with throw ropes at the ready. Just beyond the hole, the current forked around a massive boulder known as Hydro. To the left of Hydro, the current slowed into a quiet pool. To the right, it flowed to the head of Soc 'Em Dog.

"The Dog" was the most dangerous rapid on the Chattooga, a six-foot-high waterfall with a hydraulic at the bottom. At low water levels, the hydraulic was a yapping puppy, nothing to worry about even if you happened to flip. At high levels, it was a savage pit bull that would hold down any swimmer no matter how strong. High Five maintained a strict rule of portaging the rafts around Soc 'Em Dog if the water level covered a certain boulder along the far shore. Ducharme followed Annie's gaze, saw that the boulder was gone.

"Guys, we're going to be walking the Dog today," Annie said. "Make sure your people carry all their gear down to the bottom. Last time, we had two paddles left behind."

With lunch over, everyone returned to their craft. Chris and Andrew settled into their kayaks and headed on through Jawbone. Their job was to set up with ropes at the base in case anyone fell out and to signal the rafts through one at a time.

Chris appeared atop a boulder at the bottom of Jawbone. He waved his paddle overhead, a signal for Annie to come through. As he waited at the back of the line of rafts, Ducharme asked Maria if she was having fun.

She offered a half-hearted smile. "Yes."

"I hope so. We're almost done."

Chris waved on Toby and then Temo. Before he left, Temo glanced back at Ducharme, slapped his paddle across the surface and caught him full in the face.

Ducharme sputtered. "You bastard!"

Not waiting for Chris' signal, he ordered his crew to paddle full speed ahead. Charging after Temo, he maneuvered his raft around the first two turns. The speed of the current caught him by surprise and it took all of his strength to keep the raft off the boulders. Temo, too, was having trouble, plunging into the final drop at an angle. The raft rose sideways out of the hole, teetered at the top of the wave and capsized.

Ducharme yelled. "All back!"

Heads popped up in the swirling water. Ropes flew out from shore. He veered to the right to avoid running over the upside down raft. That put him dead on course to hit Hydro.

"Left side back! Right side forward!"

The girls paddled hard, but it was no use. The raft hit the big boulder sideways and rode up against the rock.

"High side!"

His order sent the crew scrambling to hold on to the high side of the raft. But not everyone could find a handhold. First LaToya, then Jessica, fell out of the bow. They surfaced on the left hand side of Hydro and washed into the slower water where the guides onshore threw them ropes. He didn't notice that Maria had fallen out of the stern until Andrew yelled and pointed.

"Swimmer!"

She was in the swift current to the right side of Hydro, flailing her thin arms in the wrong direction, headed straight toward Soc 'Em Dog.

|Two|

In his dream, Ducharme slept on a soft bed of needles beneath tall hemlocks. There was no wind, yet for some reason, a branch brushed against the top of his sleeping bag. Coming awake, he realized there was, in fact, something moving on his sleeping bag, crawling toward his head. By the close placement of the steps, he guessed it to be a spider—a big one. Curling his hand into a fist, he punched upward. There followed a sound like a marble dropping in the sand. He sat up and peered through the semi-darkness. Two yards distant, a tarantula the size of a tennis ball crawled across the chalk-colored ground.

He jumped out of his sleeping bag and dragged it to the other side of the fire ring. He got back inside, but lay fully awake. Head propped on his arm, he surveyed his surroundings. To the west, the square peaks of the Chisos Mountains held the first rays of the sun. Below, lay barren hills, peppered with dark green scrub. The ground around him looked like a gravel pit, rocks and more rocks.

He stood in his longjohns and wool cap. The desert air was cold, nothing like a June morning in Georgia. Reaching into his duffel bag, he put on socks and a pair of shorts. He donned a fleece jacket and stepped into his sneakers. The soil underfoot was like a dusting of snow, packed but loose. He walked over to his stove, turned on the gas and lit it with a match. He took a sip of water from a plastic jug and downed a Cymbalta pill, then poured the rest into a pan and waited for it to boil.

Save for the soft hiss of the burner, the world was silent. No birds. No wind. He poured the boiling water through a coffee filter, felt the tin cup grow warm in his hands. He opened a packet of oatmeal and mixed that with the remaining water in a tin bowl. Adding a box of raisins and a packet of sugar, his breakfast was ready.

The Chisos were now illuminated from top to bottom, end to end. Nowhere in the Southeast could you see an entire range of mountains. But here in the Big Bend of Texas, they said you could see the backbone of the world. Desolate, dramatic, devoid of people—it was just what he wanted.

And now it was time to see this river. He strode through the bushes like he would in Georgia, then jumped back in pain. What the hell! Creosote bushes weren't supposed to have thorns! He lifted the branch and there was a skinny little cactus hidden underneath. He sat down and pulled out the thorn, some part of it remaining behind.

"God damn!"

He picked at the wound until it felt clear, stood up and headed on. He crested a rise and stopped. Guidebooks had prepared him to be underwhelmed by the Rio Grande, but what lay before him looked more like a pool than a river, a reed-choked channel barely a hundred feet wide and shallow enough to wade.

But this was May in West Texas, and contrary to the East, the driest month of the year. Chris, his kayaking friend, had said late fall was the time to run the Rio

Grande. That was when upstream farmers stopped drawing water off to irrigate their crops. Anyway, he was not looking for another Chattooga. He was finished with Class IV rapids, shouted orders and screaming clients. At best, those brief, frenzied trips gave people nothing more than a rush of adrenaline, something they would forget within a week. At worst...

He pushed his palms against his forehead. In this time of so much turmoil in people's personal lives, so much ugliness in the world at large, what he wanted to do was surround his clients with beauty. Mind-blowing beauty. Not just for a minute or an hour, but for days on end, so they would know it still exists. Everything he'd read, everything he'd heard, was that a trip through the Lower Canyons promised such an experience. He would lead them through and change their lives for the better.

Mocking laughter, like a rusty hand pump, erupted on the Mexican side of the river. A small gray burro, then two, then three, emerged from the cane to feed on the riverside grass. With their big ears and sleepy eyes, they were silly looking beasts, wild descendants of domestic burros that the Spanish missionaries, soldiers, and gold diggers had brought in the 1500s. Those human conquistadores were long gone from the Big Bend, but the burros remained.

He checked his cellphone—9 am. Time to return to civilization. He shoved his sleeping bag in its case, stuffed his wool cap and fleece into the duffel bag along with the gas stove and eating utensils. These were the sum total of his worldly goods. These and the dust-covered van and trailer-load of canoes parked beside the road.

Ducharme had purchased the boats and trailer back East with the last of his savings. They were his meal ticket, his future. He loved canoes for their simplicity, a design largely unchanged since prehistoric times. They paddled well over flat water as well as rapids, and could be loaded with gear. His future clients would navigate their own way in these canoes, rather than being steered by a guide in a rubber raft. That came with certain risks, especially in whitewater, but he wanted them to feel the sense of freedom, of accomplishment, that came with paddling their own canoe.

Now, as he pulled out onto the gravel road, his fleet rolled with him. He'd changed boats, but could he change the man? All of his professional life, he'd been an employee, happy to let someone else take all the risks. Now, everything was up to him. There'd be no more fooling around, no more Robbie the pirate, Robbie the gnarly dude. Everything and everyone related to this business depended on him. His first order was finding a place to stay.

Outside of Persimmon Gap, his cellphone pinged to life with a message from the realtor in Alpine. "Come by this afternoon. I might have something for you."

Half an hour later, a cluster of roofs rose out of the Chihuahuan Desert. Alpine was the first real town he'd seen in West Texas, with hotels, restaurants, a hospital, even a university. He parked at the realty office and came through the door.

"Mr. Ducharme, how was your river?" Wes Raven was a thin, bald man who could be anywhere from forty to sixty. The dry air, the cigarettes, maybe both rendered his skin spotted and sallow.

"It was pretty low."

"That's the way it is this time of year. Plus, we don't

get the rains that we used to."

He sat at Raven's desk. "So, you've got something for me?"

"There's a man offering a place for rent over in Aintry. It's actually an old railroad depot. 'Somewhat restored,' it says here."

Raven handed him a sheet of paper. "Has an attached residence for the station master and his family. Should have the kind of storage space you're looking for."

He studied the photograph. "Where's Aintry?"

"It's 33.5 miles east of here. Nice little town."

"A long way from the river."

"No further than Alpine. Now, if you want to be right on the river, we're talking Terlingua. Down thataway, the pickings are slim and the prices are high."

He pulled at his beard. A train depot. That could be interesting.

"I'd go with you if I didn't have to hold down the fort," Raven said. "You want, I'll call him right now and tell him you're on the way."

"I guess it's worth a look."

***

The depot stood between the highway and the rail line, the once busy parking area overgrown with sage. Just as the realtor had said, the station bore the traditional one-story baggage compartment and a two-story attached residence on the far end. The owner's trailer stood across the road, surrounded by an assortment of junk, most notably a 1950s vintage hay truck and an Aeromotor windmill, not turning. As Ducharme pulled in the dirt drive, a mangy pit bull sprang out from under the trailer. He stayed in the car, letting the dog bark until the trailer door opened. An old man stuck his head out, white hair, milky blue eyes, a lined face that mirrored the eroded hills on the horizon.

"Pancho!" he yelled.

The dog retreated under the trailer. Ducharme stepped out of the car.

"You the one come to see the depot?" the man asked.

"Yes, sir."

He offered his hand, rough as a leather glove. "Name's Alfred."

"Robbie."

"Let me get the key."

Through the open door of the trailer, Ducharme could hear Fox News on the TV. Newspapers and magazines were stacked in front of a yellow sofa, stuffing coming out the top. Alfred caught him looking, pulled the door closed.

"I don't usually have guests," he said.

Pancho came slinking out from under the trailer, subdued this time. He leaned his nose into Ducharme's leg.

"He won't bother you," Alfred said. "You ain't Mexican."

"He knows the difference?"

Alfred gave him a look. "Don't you?"

On bowed legs, the old man wound his way through the yard and stopped at the edge of the road.

"Watch yourself crossing. We don't have much traffic, but every now and then someone'll blow by at 90 miles an hour. Supposed to slow down to 35 going through town."

Visible a block away, the town consisted of a string of one-story adobe buildings connected by a wooden awning and a sidewalk. Ducharme had glimpsed a laundromat driving through, a novelty store, and a café. None of them looked open.

"You a river guide?" Alfred said.

"Yes, sir."

"I can tell by the hair. No one else wears it long in these parts. Too hot."

As he crossed the street, Ducharme took the depot's measure. Except for the faded lettering bearing the name "Aintry," the structure was unpainted.

"It's all cypress," Alfred said. "All the old stations were made of cypress. Never rots, especially out here."

"How come it's got an attached residence?"

"My understanding is the railroad needed to do that to get anyone to take the job. No one wanted to live way the hell out here. Most people still don't."

"How old is the building?"

"Built around 1885, abandoned in 1964. I bought it for $25,000. Thought I might live here when I still had a family."

Alfred stopped in front of the baggage room and lifted the latch on one of the two bay doors.

"Do these doors lock?" Ducharme asked. "I'd like to store my canoes and camping equipment in here and I can't afford to have anything stolen."

"They lock if you put one on 'em."

The rusted wheels creaked across the top rail. Inside, beams of sunlight shone down through ragged holes in the ceiling, illuminating a large, empty space. The floor was covered in some kind of droppings.

"Do you have raccoons or something in here?"

"That's owl shit. There's a family of Great Horneds that get in through the holes in the ceiling. I've been meaning to fix that roof."

He hoisted himself up to the sill and walked across the room. An old metal-wheeled baggage cart stood against one wall. On another, he found parts to a double-sized brass bed. He ran his hand over the sculpted pineapples atop the posts.

"That I got at an antique auction," Alfred said. "I was hoping I could use it, but it don't fit in the trailer."

Alfred stood while he stared around the room. "You ready to see the rest?"

Through a side door, a short hallway ran past the ticket office and into the waiting room. There was an old rolltop desk in the ticket office and four benches in the waiting room. The tongue-and-groove walls and ceiling looked to be in good condition. But at ten in the morning, it was already stifling hot.

"Do these windows open?"

"Might take some work, but they'll open."

"I take it I couldn't put in air conditioning."

Alfred shook his head. "It's all two-pronged outlets. You can get by with a fan most days."

He led the way to the living quarters upstairs. "Stairway's creaky, but it'll hold your weight."

At the top of the stairs, a door opened onto a small bathroom with a toilet, a sink, and a water-stained claw foot tub. Ducharme turned one of the handles. The spigot coughed then emitted a stream of brown water.

"It'll clear in a minute," Alfred said.

A short hallway led to a narrow kitchen on one side and a bedroom on the other. Both were covered with dust, but otherwise in good shape. Alfred opened the door at the end of the hall.

"This used to be the living room. It's got windows on three sides. Gets a nice cross-breeze at night."

Ducharme paused to take in the ten-foot-high ceiling, the hardwood floor, and the fireplace with the tile surround. This room had definite possibilities.

He walked to the south-facing window, stared out at the treeless plain. In the middle distance, an umber capped cindercone rose to a pale blue sky.

"Is that a volcano?" he said.

"Used to be. About a million years ago."

"Wow."

He crossed to the north-facing windows.

"Those are your Glass Mountains over there," Alfred said.

"How about to the east?"

"Nothing but desert all the way to the Pecos River. Some people call it a semi-arid steppe. I call it a desert."

This could make a fantastic bedroom. Put in a ceiling fan and position a bed against the wall...he walked again to the south-facing window and stared down at the tracks. "How often does a train pass?"

"Twice a day. Once around noon and then about ten at night. It'll scare the hell out of you the first couple of times. I don't even hear it anymore."

He turned around. "Would you mind if I commandeered that bed downstairs?"

"Suit yourself. It's just gathering dust." Alfred waited at the door. "Well, that's about it."

Decision time. He agonized for a long minute. The depot needed a lot of work. Maybe he should keep looking. But he had a trailer load of canoes to store, equipment to buy, and a business to start.

"When did you say you're going to fix that roof?"

"Soon as I can find someone to do it."

"What would you think about letting me stay a few months for free in exchange for fixing the roof? I'm kind of in a bind for cash until my business gets going."

"Lemme see your hands."

Ducharme hesitated, extended his arms. Alfred turned them palms up. "Looks like you've spent some time swinging a hammer," he said. "You've got a deal."

|Three|

Janey Hart scanned the Canyonland Adventures application and stopped on Question 4—Marital Status. Why on earth did her marital status matter? Would she be deemed a better canoeist if she were married? Or was it the other way around? In any case, it was none of their business. But if she left it blank, they might reject her application. "Married" was technically the right term, though that was likely not to be true by the time the trip started. And the thought of identifying herself as still married to Worth, her soon-to-be ex-husband, was disgusting. "Single" had its appeal, but whomever saw that her daughter was also coming on the trip would suspect that she was actually divorced. Or had never been married. She decided on "N/A."

Question 5 was also disturbing—List Medications You Are Currently Taking. She understood the medical justification for this, but one could easily misconstrue the kind of person she was. She took Cymbalta for depression. Would this guy—she was sure it was a man—assume she could not be depended on to do her duties? Would he think she needed to be treated with extra care? The Fosamax she took for retaining bone density should not be an issue. Or would he fear she might break an arm or leg on the trip?

The chlorthalidone she took for hypertension could also leave her suspect. All told, the drugs made her seem a mental and physical wreck, though at 42, she was in physically good shape. She worked out three days a week, trying, originally for Worth's sake, to keep her figure. Now, she did it as a matter of pride. She was not going to let herself go, the way so many divorcees around her age did.

Question 6—Regular Exercise. That was easy. Fitness center, three days a week, one hour per session.

Question 7—Describe Your Paddling Experience (list rivers and their American Whitewater Association ratings). The ratings, she recalled, were based on the degree of difficulty of the rapids—Class I-V. Class I rapids were easy—basically just ripples. Class II rapids might have some bouncy waves or some rocks that had to be dodged, but nothing hazardous. Class III rapids had big waves that could swamp a canoe or rocks that had to be dodged lest you pin your canoe against them. Beyond that she'd never run and wasn't interested in trying.

In their early years of marriage, while living in Atlanta, she and Worth had canoed the Chattahoochee River many times. Or maybe it was just two. They had argued each time, hit many rocks, but they had never tipped over. The "Hooch," she remembered, was considered a Class II river. And they had run the Nantahala River in western North Carolina. That was rated a Class II, though there was one Class III rapid, Nantahala Falls, and they had tipped over on that. Should she admit that they capsized and that Worthless said it was her fault for not paddling hard enough in the bow? This happened in front of hordes of people watching from the bank. She was so shocked by the

55-degree water that she failed to respond to the rescue rope thrown from shore. The crowd was howling "grab the rope, grab the rope," but it wasn't until she had banged her ass on a rock and came to her senses that she spotted the yellow line across her legs. She closed her hands around it and was dragged to shore like a dead fish, there to be berated by her husband.

"Nantahala River," she wrote defiantly. "Class III."

She went to the refrigerator and poured herself a glass of wine. It was only Monday, but already she had a headache. She went to the bottom of the stairs and called to her daughter.

"Lara?"

No answer.

"Lara, are you up there?"

Her response, when it came, was dripping with insult. "What?"

"Have you done that application for the canoe trip?"

No answer.

"Lara?"

"No."

"I'd like you to do it tonight, so I can mail yours and mine back tomorrow."

"I'm doing homework."

"Can I fill it out for you?"

"Fine."

"I'm coming up."

Lara sat on the bed with her long legs crossed, her straight, blonde hair touching the laptop. She had nearly outgrown the twin bed she'd slept in as a child, but there was no room for anything larger. She needed all the floor space she could get to throw her dirty clothes.

"It's on the desk," she said.

Janey moved aside notebooks and papers until she found the folded blue-green form. She spread it out and began to fill in the blanks—age, 15; height, 5'9"; weight, ...

"How much do you weigh, Lara?"

"I have no idea."

"You filled out a physical for the swim team. What did you put?"

"I don't know. 115."

She had added a little weight since the fall, her bra size finally going from a 32 B to a C. "I'll put 120."

"Whatever."

Medications. She would put down the Cymbalta. This man might as well know Lara was on antidepressants. It might help him to understand her moodiness. But she was not going to put down the Valtrex. It made her sick to know that her 15-year-old daughter already had herpes, and she wasn't going to let the world hear about it.

Exercise. Swim team. Five days a week, two hours per day, twelve months a year. She doubted anyone on the trip could equal that.

Paddling Experience. "Didn't you canoe at Camp Riverlea?" she asked.

"It was in a pond."

"But you went down the Green River, right?"

"I guess so."

"Were there any rapids?"

"I don't know. What does it matter?"

"They want to know about your river running experience. They want a rating, which I know you don't know. "

"There were some rapids. Some of them were pretty

big."

"I'm going to put Class II."

Lara sat up and brushed back her hair. "What is this trip again?"

Janey sighed. "It's a canoe trip down the Rio Grande in Texas. We talked about this."

"And when are we going?"

"December. At the start of your Christmas break."

"How long is it?"

"We'll be gone a week. Five days are on the river."

"A *week*?"

"Yes. We discussed this."

"God! Is there going to be anybody my age on this trip?"

"I hope so."

"It better not be just old people."

It took everything Janey had not to scream. Worth had been mean to her, but he had his reasons. Lara, on the other hand, had received nothing but love from the day she was born. Anyone else who showed this kind of rudeness would be tossed out of the house, or at least given a firm lecture. But she could not do that with Lara.

With the end of her marriage, she had to decide what was meaningful in her life, what she could control and what not. She could do nothing about resurrecting her marriage and, for the time being, could not seem to reach her oldest daughter. But she could re-establish her bond with Lara. The Canyonlands Adventures website described the Lower Canyons as a trip of a lifetime. Winning Lara's trust and affection would make that dream come true.

As she walked down the hall, Janey thought to look in the attic for the camping gear. Worth could reach the pull cord for the drop staircase, but at 5'8" she could not. She took the stool from Lara's bathroom—a leftover from childhood—and set it beneath the trap door. Bits of insulation rained down as she opened the door and unfolded the steps. She climbed gingerly upward, felt the blast of heat as she entered the attic. Old suitcases and cardboard boxes were packed on the flooring between the insulation. There were two sleeping bags, hers and Lara's. She threw them down the stairs and searched for the tent. It was nowhere to be found.

"Lara, did you take the tent for some reason?"

"No. Why would I?"

She tossed the suitcases aside. Fucking Worth. That tent was a present to both of them from her parents. He might not have remembered that, but he had no right to take it without asking. This was the horrible division of stuff that her friends had warned her about.

She turned to climb down and there, wedged in with the suitcases, was the tent.

No sooner had she folded the applications and sealed the envelope than fears flooded her mind. Was she asking too much of Lara on this mother-daughter trip? How would her daughter take being deprived of friends? Would she act up or just be sullen and morose? Either way, the others on the trip would think Lara a brat and her a terrible mother. It could be a disaster.

|Four|

The last thunderclap rolled out of the Davis Mountains and onto the West Texas plains. In the bunkhouse, Danny Gallagher finished waxing the ends of his white handlebar moustache, set his felt cowboy hat on his balding head, and stepped out the door. The air temperature had dropped 20 degrees with the passing storm and the oaks in the yard of the Leaton Ranch sparkled with raindrops. It was going to be a fine day.

In the equipment shed, Gallagher settled into the seat of his camo green Kawasaki ATV. He loved this 4-wheeler as much as any horse he'd ever ridden. It was much easier on his 65-year-old body and had conveniences you couldn't mount on a saddle—drink holder, CB radio... He clicked on the radio, and spoke in his high, thin voice. "This is Danny. I'm headed out to fix that fence."

Mrs. Leaton's voice crackled back. "You're just leaving now?"

"Yes, ma'am. That storm just cleared."

"10-4."

He started the engine and headed out the track that rose into the tree-spotted hills. Biologists called the Davis Mountains a "sky island," isolated terrain filled with all kinds of plants and animals not found in the surrounding region. In the middle of July when the blush of spring in the rest of the state was a distant memory, the trees in the Davis were as green as a store-bought lizard. Gallagher was tickled to work here, surrounded by all this beauty.

The pay wasn't much. Mrs. Leaton had what they call short arms and deep pockets. In fact, after a series of layoffs, he was the only hired hand on this 7,000-acre ranch. So he wasn't about to hurry on any of the endless tasks he was assigned.

Halfway up the mountain, he spotted something. Across the valley, equal in elevation to where he sat, was a big, flat-topped boulder. There was something round on top of that boulder that wasn't usually there. He pulled out his binoculars and glassed the hillside.

"I'll be goddamned," he said. "This is my lucky day."

The round spot was the head of a mountain lion sunning on top of the rock. This was only the second time in ten years he'd seen a mountain lion here, and the other time, it was running away. This one sat there looking at him without a care in the world.

He shut off the engine.

"You are a cocky one. Top of that rock is like a big ol' couch. I'll bet you've got a bellyful of mule deer. Mess with those cows, I'm going to have to shoot you. Yes, sir, I'll be watching."

He set the glasses down, picked them up again. This was an opportunity not to be missed. Fifteen minutes passed and the cat still hadn't moved.

"Alright, missy, church is out. I'm going to have to head on down the road."

He drove on over the ridge, the ATV bucking over the stony path. Down into a draw on the far side, he came to one of the water tanks set out for cattle. This was his favorite spot on the ranch, a little Shangri La shaded by orange-barked madrone trees, a spring burbling out of a rock outcropping, the water fed through a pipe straight into the tank. He rolled up his sleeve and checked the bottom for sediment. Not too bad.

Out from beneath the oaks came an old longhorn bull.

"Look who we've got here. Mr. Bocephus. Do you think I have something for you? Yes, I do."

He reached for the feedbag in the bed of the ATV and tossed some thumb-sized pellets on the ground. The bull walked forward on stiff legs and lapped them up.

Gallagher broke into a Hank Williams song about not being loved like you used to. The bull looked mournfully back. His horns still had that magnificent spread, but his eyes were rheumy and his haunches thin.

"You're not long for this world are you, my friend?" Danny said. "You've had your time with the ladies, just like old Danny. Pretty soon, we're going to take you to town and give you the hot shot. Those horns will end up on some rich man's mantelpiece."

He wiped a tear from his eye. "I swear."

The CB crackled to life. "Danny, are you there?"

He picked up the handset. "Yes, ma'am."

"Have you fixed that fence yet?"

"No, ma'am. I'm checking on the water tank."

"You need to fix that fence before any more cows get out."

"Yes, ma'am."

"And come by the office after you get back."

He didn't like the sound of that. She'd been short with him of late, saying he was taking too much time on his chores. Let her try keeping up with 7,500 acres!

He drove along the fence line until he found the broken strand of barbed wire. He got out the fence stretcher and clamped it to the ends. He ratcheted the wire tight, slipped the wires into a sleeve and squeezed it tight with a crimping tool. Trim the loose ends and the job was done.

Fifteen minutes later, he was back at the ranch.

"You wouldn't believe what I just saw," he said as he came through the office door. Mrs. Leaton, behind her desk, glanced to his right. Somebody was sitting on a chair against the wall—swarthy skin, black hair, Stetson hat—a Mexican.

"Danny, this is Javier," she said. "I was hoping to talk with you before he came, but you were late as usual."

The Mexican averted his eyes. Gallagher felt the boulder coming down the mountain.

"Danny, I don't know if it's your age or your attitude, but your work ethic is not what it used to be," Mrs. Leaton said. "I'm going to have to let you go. Javier is going to be taking your place."

He stood dumbfounded.

"I'll give you two weeks with pay to find another place to live and work. I hope you'll use that time to show Javier the ropes. There'll be a nice retirement check at the end of it."

He turned to the Mexican. "Are you a U.S. citizen, sir?"

"That's none of your business," Mrs. Leaton said.

"I bet he ain't even legal. I bet his boots are still wet from crossing the river. What are you paying him, $10 an hour?"

"Danny!"

He sniffed. "Fuck me. I'll take that check now."

Mrs. Leaton opened the drawer. "I really hate to end things this way, but if that's the way you want it..." She pulled out a checkbook and wrote him a check. "Thanks for all you've done. Best of luck."

He took the check—$2,000—and stormed out the door. Back in the bunkhouse, he threw all of his belongings in an old Army duffel bag—four pearl snap shirts, two pairs of jeans, assorted T-shirts, underwear, socks, and a Ruger P95 pistol.

"I ain't gonna work with no Mexican," he said to no one. "And you ain't gonna fire me. I quit!"

Behind the wheel of his Ford F150, Gallagher shot gravel across the ranch house yard. He pulled onto the paved road and headed east, crying like a baby all the way to Fort Davis.

***

The Hotel Limpia had the only bar in town, frequented mostly by the retired tourist crowd. They were all at the tables, laughing it up, celebrating the easy life. Gallagher took a seat at the bar.

Emilio, dressed in his fashionable black shirt and pants, opened the fridge and held up a Bud Light. "The usual?"

He shook his head. "I'll have a tall margarita. Make that with Herradura Silver."

Emilio raised an eyebrow. "Did you get a raise?"

"Nope. I quit. I don't work for *no one* for $10 an hour."

Emilio mixed the drink in a silver shaker and poured it into a glass. "What are you going to do now?"

"Hell if I know." Turning halfway around on his stool,

he addressed the tourists. "The owners are only hiring goddamned *Mexicans*. All they care about is the *bottom line*."

Faces looked up from the tables.

"Careful, amigo," Emilio said.

"I'm not talking about you," he said. "You're one of the good ones."

He drained his glass and pushed it across the bar. "Pour me another and I'll shut the hell up."

By closing time, he was falling down drunk. He made it back to his truck and passed out in the seat.

In the morning, there came a tap on the window. He opened one eye. Sheriff Thomas.

"Roll this window down, please."

Gallagher cranked down the window. "Good morning, officer."

"What are you doing here, Danny? Aren't you supposed to be at work?"

"Sir, I quit."

The sheriff frowned. "Well, you can't stay here."

He sat up and rubbed his face. Tears welled in his eyes. "I don't know, sheriff. I just don't know."

"I'm not going to run you off right away. But you can't stay here another night."

He took a deep breath, started the engine. "Well, adios, amigo. You won't see me around no more."

The sheriff tapped the door. "Don't do anything foolish."

|Five|

The air horn blew at the edge of town, followed by the faint thrumming of the diesel engines. The sound grew louder until the ground beneath the old train depot shook. By the time the engines flew past, twenty feet from his bed, Ducharme was fully awake. Now came the screaming of the wheels, a beast being dragged to a horrible death. He got up and turned on the shower, shampooed his long hair, hung his head, and squeezed it clear. By the time he stepped out, the last car was clicking away in the distance.

He dressed in shorts and a T-shirt, went downstairs and stepped out onto the wooden platform. The boards were cracked from a century-and-a-half of desert sun and air. Across the tracks, the sere landscape was baking in the white light of another cloudless day. In the two months Ducharme had been here, it had scarcely rained a drop. His nasal passages felt like pine cones, the skin on his arms scaled like a lizard. And summer was supposed to be the rainy season.

Rumor had it that the climate in West Texas had changed for good, that rainfall would be nonexistent, save for violent storms that swept in off the Gulf. Those storms might raise the level of the local rivers several feet, but only for a matter of hours. Then, they would recede and the mud banks crack like broken pottery.

He began to feel that his plans were for naught, that leading canoe trips down the Rio Grande would be limited to two months, maybe three, not nearly enough to support an outfitting business. He would have to supplement this with something else—backpacking trips in Big Bend National Park, sightseeing tours in his van. He was less excited about these and unsure of the demand. What if he failed altogether? He couldn't go back to Georgia, couldn't ask his aging parents for help.

Every week he suffered nightmares. In the aftermath of the accident on the Chattooga, he was back at the High Five Base Camp, called into the owner's office to provide an explanation. He knew the accident wasn't his fault, but somehow he couldn't find the right words. He called in the other guides to back his story up, but for some reason, they would not, offering contradictory stories about what had happened. He was fired, cast out of the family he'd known and loved for a decade. Wandering through a strange desert, he called out for help, but no one answered. He knew he was going to die.

Ducharme awoke in a sweat, the flaking plaster of the bedroom ceiling coming into focus. He needed to get some professional help, but there was no such thing as a psychotherapist in the windblown streets of Aintry. And he had to be very careful about talking to anyone else. The Big Bend was a small community and if word got out about the accident on the Chattooga, his outfitting business on the Rio Grande might never get off the ground.

He picked up the keys to the van and headed to town. Even if he couldn't share his inner-most fears, he had to talk to someone he knew. In Aintry, that would be the postmaster or the waitress at the Pronghorn Cafe.

Christian Foushee, Aintry's postmaster general, was, as far as Ducharme could tell, the only African-American in Brewster County, Texas. In the 19th century, there'd been many blacks serving in the U.S. Army, chasing down Apaches and Comanches from the headquarters of the Ninth Cavalry at Fort Davis. But the fort had closed in the early 1900s and most of the occupants had settled elsewhere. Foushee was not related to any of these servicemen, but Ducharme enjoyed joking with him, calling him the last of the Buffalo Soldiers.

"Good morning, Captain Christian," Ducharme said as he came through the post office door. "Are we holding down the fort?"

"Yes, sir, Mr. Ducharme. No sign of Indians."

"Then it must be a good day."

"It could be a good day for you. I just put a letter in your box."

"Really?"

This day, July 30, was the deadline Ducharme had set for applications to be mailed in for the third of his four planned fall/winter canoe trips down the Lower Canyons of the Rio Grande. He'd filled up the first two trips and had received half-a-dozen applications for his third. Four of these applicants—three men and a woman—were realtors from Cary, North Carolina, and two were a mother and daughter from Atlanta. He needed one more person to meet his minimum quota of seven. He opened his box and took out the envelope. A blue-green application lay folded inside.

"I think we have a winner," he said.

"I told you."

He held up the application to confirm his hopes. In an instant, his depression lifted. The trip was on.

"This deserves a breakfast burrito at the Pronghorn," he said.

"Go for it, Mr. Ducharme."

Angelina Ortega, the twenty-year-old waitress at the town's only cafe, had a sweet smile and gorgeous eyes. But she had no interest in life beyond Aintry. Try as he might, Ducharme could not engage her in a conversation of any substance.

"Just coffee for you, Mr. Ducharme?" she said.

He shook his head. "Today, I'm going to have one of your breakfast burritos."

She wrote down his order.

"I'm feeling lucky today," he said. "I just filled out my third trip down the Rio Grande."

"That's nice." She poured his coffee. "I'll have that burrito right out."

He opened the application and scanned the information. "Janko Dagic." Was that pronounced *Dagick* or *Dagich*?

The man was 55 years old, 6'1" and 190 pounds—a big guy. Hopefully, he could paddle stern in one of the four canoes.

Marital status—"Single." Current medications— "None." He doubted that, but if Mr. Dagic chose to hide his weaknesses, that was his concern.

Paddling Experience—"Black River, Class III." There were Black Rivers all over the country, but none that he was aware of with that kind of rating. Dagic was from Chicago, hardly the land of whitewater rivers. He'd have to ask him about that when they met.

Angelina brought the burrito—a Pronghorn specialty with scrambled egg, bits of bacon, onions, chilis, cheese, and potatoes. He'd have to add this to his trip breakfasts.

"Anything else for you, Mr. Ducharme?"

"How are you doing today?"

"Fine."

That was the extent of any of their conversations. "Yes. No. Fine."

"Has your daughter started camp?"

"Yes, she's enjoying it very much."

"That's good. Well, I'll let you go."

Back at the depot, Ducharme put Dagic's application in the file, considered how this man might fit in with the others. The success of these multi-day trips depended upon personalities as much as paddling skills. One bad egg could spoil the trip for everyone.

He left the office and opened the door to the baggage compartment. The holes in the roof were gone thanks to his month-long repair and re-shingling job, never to be attempted again. His knees took weeks to recover, but at least there were no more invading owls. He sorted through the camping gear to make sure he had sleeping bags, pads, and tents. Still on order was a plastic toilet seat to go on top of the "honey pot." Aside from that, there was nothing to do but wait.

He climbed the stairs to the kitchen and made himself a canned tuna sandwich. He checked his phone for messages, started a game of solitaire and abandoned it. He stared out the window. Nothing to see, nothing to do, no one to speak to, nowhere to go. Back at High Five, he lived amidst the bustle of the bunkhouse, the boat barn, and the river. Here, there was only silence. And the scuffling of mice. Since the day he'd moved in, he'd heard their scribbling feet in the walls, glimpsed them stealing along the edges of the kitchen and bedroom. He was not afraid of mice, but wished them gone. He had enough demons invading his mind.

That night, his dreams were shattered by a high-pitched yowl. He went to the window and saw a Great Horned Owl hovering over the scrubby yard. Something was down there in the darkness. He grabbed a flashlight and went out into the yard. The giant owl held its ground, hovering twenty feet over a creosote bush. Whatever he was after, he hadn't caught it yet. Ducharme aimed his flashlight low to the ground. Crouched beneath the bush was a small cat, clearly injured. He called to it, but it hissed and backed away.

There was no escape for the wounded creature. The owl would wait as long as it had to. If he was going to rescue the cat, he had to act now. Removing his shirt, he got down on all fours and crawled forward. Before the cat could escape, he threw his shirt over it, pinned it to the ground, and carried it inside.

Upstairs in the bedroom, he set the cat on the floor. The owl had clearly gotten hold of it, leaving a set of bloody puncture wounds across its back. The cat dragged itself under the bed, where it mewed pathetically. He went to the kitchen, poured milk in a bowl, and set it on the floor. The cat stayed put. Tired of waiting, he slipped back into bed.

Somewhere in the night, he dreamed of a woman licking his ear in a clear attempt at seduction. He woke to discover the cat on his shoulder, its raspy tongue digging at his ear wax. The animal stared at him through crusted eyes. It was a young cat, beyond a kitten, very likely born in the wild. He needed to get it to a vet if it was going to live.

At first light, he crossed the street and rapped on the trailer door. Alfred appeared in his usual disheveled state, white hair standing on his head.

"There is one vet in town," he said. "It's that red house with the cypress trees on 4th Street. Just knock."

Ducharme knew those trees—two arrow-straight Italian cypress taller than anything else in town. He'd never paid attention to the house, but, now, as he pulled into the driveway, he saw clear evidence of female habitation—rose-colored adobe walls and a sky blue door.

Carmen Gomez was young for Aintry, no more than 30. She had a pretty face—large eyes, full lips, and eyebrows that could have been penciled in. Her hands, holding the door as she looked up, were long and smooth. He explained he was the guy renting the old train depot at the other end of town.

"Oh, yes, I know who you are," Carmen said. "I'm glad someone is finally fixing it up."

"I've got an injured cat in the car. Do you have time to look at it?"

"Bring it inside. I've got a room in the back."

Carmen's living room doubled as a waiting room, with pet med brochures in plastic stands on the tables. She led him through to the operating room, a 10 x 12 aqua-painted room with cinderblock walls and a linoleum floor. He set the cat on the examining table. Carmen bent over and spoke in a gentle voice.

"It's O.K.," she said. "I'm not going to hurt you."

The cat arched its back and hissed.

"This is a bad looking injury," she said. "How did this happen?"

He explained that the cat was attacked by an owl during the night. "She needs stitches, right? I hope it's not too late."

"It depends on whether any of these punctures has gotten to an inner organ."

She opened a wall cabinet and got out antiseptic, wipes, and an electric razor.

"Is this your cat or is it wild?" she said.

"It's wild. But I'd like it to be mine if we can fix it up. I've got a mouse problem."

"The reason I ask is that this will cost you quite a bit if it's yours. If it's wild, I can fix it for free."

"I guess you have your answer."

He liked the tone of authority in her voice. She was confident in dealing with customers and, hopefully, with wounded animals.

"Do you have a name for her?" she said. "It's a she, you know."

"I don't. Not yet. What's the Spanish word for 'lucky'?"

"Suerte."

"That doesn't have much of a ring to it."

"'Lucky one' is 'afortunado.'"

"Afortunado. How about we call her 'Tunado' for short."

"That works for me."

He looked away as Carmen gave Tunado a shot to kill the pain. On the wall was a Pre-Veterinary degree from Sul Ros State in Alpine, and a Veterinary degree from Texas A&M.

"A&M. Are you one of the football crazies?" he asked.

She laughed. A good sign. "No. Graduate students aren't required to attend. And, believe me, I didn't."

She cleaned Tunado's wounds with antiseptic and then began shaving her with an electric razor.

"So what are you doing in Aintry?" he said. "Doesn't seem like there'd be much business here."

"You'd be surprised. There are over 60 cats in this town and half as many dogs. Then, there are all the cattle, horses, and goats out on the ranches. What are *you* doing here?" she said.

"I'm setting up a guiding business on the Rio Grande. Canyonlands Adventures."

"You look like a river guide."

He assumed she was talking about his beard. Her tone suggested that she, like Alfred, considered it out of place.

She probed each of the cat's wounds and declared they had not penetrated an organ. She stitched the holes slowly and efficiently, a turn-on for Ducharme. He couldn't see her full figure through the lab coat, but she wasn't flat chested. And she wasn't wearing a ring.

The stitching done, Carmen handed him the cat. "Keep her quiet for 24 hours," she said.

"Can I pay you something?"

"No. Like I said, I treat wild cats for free."

"O.K. Can I invite you to dinner?"

She gave him a sultry smile. "That would be nice."

"How about tomorrow?"

The next morning, he drove to Fort Stockton and bought a pair of plastic Adirondack chairs to set out on the platform, a rug for the bedroom, groceries, and two bottles of wine. He swept the mouse shit off the floors and cleaned the bathroom and kitchen.

Carmen's appearance at the door rendered him momentarily speechless. She wore red lipstick, abalone earrings, a peasant blouse and tight-fitting jeans. How had this person existed in this town for two months without his knowing?

"Welcome to the depot," he said.

"Look who's here!"

Tunado appeared at the edge of the doorway, seemingly recovered from her encounter with the owl. Carmen knelt down, revealing deep cleavage. And a gold necklace with a crucifix hanging in between. Bummer. For one, it meant she believed in something he did not. And in these parts, it meant she was probably a Catholic. If she was religious, there'd be no sex outside of marriage.

Just as quickly as Tunado had appeared, she slipped through Carmen's hands and disappeared into the yard.

"Oh, no. I'm so sorry," Carmen said. "Put some food out for her. She'll come back."

He sighed. "She'll have to make it on her own. Or not. Come on in and I'll give you the tour."

He started with the waiting room, its walls decorated with various treasures he'd rescued from the yard, including the rotor blade from Alfred's windmill and the grill from the Reo hay truck.

She ran her fingers across the speckled chrome. "Where did you find this?"

"That came off of one of Alfred's trucks. He said I have to give it back if he ever fixes it up."

"That will never happen," she said. "Those things have been rusting in his yard ever since I moved here."

She peered through the ticket window into the station master's office, topographic maps and books about the Big

Bend strewn across the rolltop desk.

"That's my office now," he said. "You can tell by the mess."

"This is so cool. You're really putting this place to use."

"Wait'll you see the upstairs."

He led the way up the creaking staircase to the kitchen, its stovetop covered with bubbling pots.

"Mmm, it smells good in here. What are you making us?"

"Chicken curry, green beans sautéed in garlic and almonds, a mixed green salad."

"Impressive."

He went to the end of the hall and opened the door to the bedroom. "Then, there's this."

Carmen walked into the center of the room and stood with her hands on her hips. She lifted one heel and turned halfway around, silhouetting pretty legs and a great ass.

"This is killing me," she said. "You have views in three directions. And a brass bed."

"That's also a loaner from Alfred. I had to go to Fort Stockton to find a mattress that would fit it."

She ran her hand across the comforter. "Very nice."

Back in the kitchen, he sat her at the metal table with a glass of rosé and finished cooking dinner.

"How is it that you're such a gourmand?" she said. "A river guide like you."

"I'm a guide, but I'm also the cook," he said. "People rate river companies a lot on their food, so I'm making a point of learning a bunch of different dishes."

"And how are you rated?"

"Out here, I'm an unknown. It'll take me awhile to build up a reputation." He smiled. "You could help by spreading the word."

She smiled back. "We'll see."

They carried their dinner downstairs and out to the platform. He poured a glass of wine for Carmen and one for himself. The sun had gone down behind the depot and the temperature had dropped back into the 80s. To the south, a thunderstorm arose, lightning flashing from the belly of a long, black cloud. Rain hung like a bridal veil, never quite touching the ground. The storm traveled across the sky until it ran out of steam, the cloud dispersing into the blue.

"Wow, you never see anything like that in Georgia," he said. "A storm being born, traveling across the sky, and dying. I guess that's a Western thing."

She studied his face. "You're not the usual asocial type that moves to Aintry. How come you don't live down in Terlingua with the other guides?"

He shrugged. "It's expensive down there. And I don't really like hanging out with other guides. Too much shop talk."

"A guide who doesn't like to hang out with other guides? That seems strange."

As the sun left the top of the volcano, they began to talk about their earlier lives. Carmen's ancestors had been ranchers near El Paso in the early 1800s when it was part of the Mexican Provincia de Nuevo Mexico. They struggled to keep the Apaches from stealing their cows and horses, finally relocating south of the river. The family had continued ranching for three more generations, she emigrating to the States in her teens to attend college.

Ducharme talked about his middle class upbringing in Atlanta, his father a lawyer and his mother a school administrator. He reminisced about his days at summer camps in the Southern Appalachians, learning how to backpack and canoe.

"You didn't have to work in summer?" Carmen said.

"No, not as a teenager."

"I worked every summer," Carmen said. "I helped my father around our ranch. That's where I came to love working with animals."

Carmen asked if he'd gone to college. He winced.

"I went, but I dropped out. I just couldn't keep up with the work. I guess I'm ADD."

"Do you take drugs?" she asked.

"Yes, but there's still a lot of stuff I forget to do. I have to constantly remind myself."

"You got a job as a guide back in Georgia. How long did you work there?"

"Ten years."

"Why'd you leave?"

"I had some issues with my boss. Plus, I wanted to start my own business."

"So you moved all the way out here without knowing a soul. Without even having seen the river!"

He gave a sheepish smile. Whether she was impressed or thought him a fool, he couldn't tell.

He held up the empty bottle of wine. "Shall I get us another?"

"No, I think I'm going to head on home," she said. "This has been wonderful, thank you."

His heart sank. Things were going so well. Why did she want to leave? Maybe this was as much as he could expect on a first "date." He rose and followed her out to her car. She turned and smiled. He was certain she wanted to be kissed. He held her waist and softly pressed his lips to hers. She didn't pull away, but she didn't kiss back.

"Have I done something wrong?" he said.

"No, I just don't like men with all this hair."

He pulled back. His hair. Most of the women he'd met loved his hair. But not Carmen. Maybe it was an Hispanic thing.

"Would you like this man better if he didn't have all this hair?" he said.

"I might."

Wow, this was serious. He'd had long hair and a beard for more than a decade. It was a part of his identity as a freewheeling soul, a river man. Who would he be without it?

"I don't know of any barbers in Aintry," he said.

"You know me."

"Are you any good?"

"I shave animals all the time."

He pondered his options.

"So when would you want to do this?" he said.

"How about next Saturday?"

The next week, Carmen arrived carrying a pair of scissors, a straight edge and an electric razor.

"Let's do this in the bathroom," she said. "It's going to be messy."

They climbed the stairs and got a straight back chair to set before the mirror.

"How short should we cut it?" he asked.

"Why don't we cut it very short and you can let it grow back as much as you like? Take off your shirt."

He pulled his t-shirt off and dropped it on the floor, his bronze, muscled chest reflected in the mirror. She draped a towel over his shoulders.

"Here we go."

She lifted his locks and began to cut. With each click of the scissors, thick clumps of hair fell to the floor. It was torture to watch the change, but he vowed to withhold judgment until she was done. She put the scissors down and started in on his beard with the electric razor. Curly-cued hair fell on his chest and lap.

"Now, let's wet your face," she said.

She ran hot water in the sink, soaked a washcloth and dabbed it on his stubble. She shot a dab of shaving cream in her hand and spread it over his face. Lifting his chin with a firm hand, she shaved him with the straight edge. He hadn't felt air on the lower part of his face in ages. He felt naked, exposed.

Wiping the cream away with the cloth, she stopped to admire her work. "We're close."

She shaved the back of his neck and brushed his two-inch-long hair backward.

"There," she said. "What do you think?"

He stared at the elongated head and dimpled chin. "Weird. Very weird."

"It's going to take some getting used to."

She gathered her equipment and left the room. He continued to stare at the face in the mirror. It was the face of a man of 35, but the grey-blue eyes, peering out from beneath hooded lids, belonged to someone older. Someone hurting. Anyone could see that now. He tapped the top of his head, felt the short, stiff hair like a bristle brush against his palm. He lifted the towel from his shoulders and wiped the last of the shaving cream from his neck.

Carmen came back in the room. He was aware of her

presence, but not until she came up behind him and laid her breasts across his shoulders did he realize she was naked. The sight of those dark-nippled orbs in the mirror, their warmth and weight on his skin, sent a jolt of electricity through his veins. She ran her fingers down his arms, whispered in his ear, "I think you look very handsome."

He broke into a boyish smile. Never had he been so surprised, so humored, so aroused.

She led him into the bedroom and laid down on the covers. He stripped off his clothes and lowered himself on top of her. He entered her slowly, like a child enters a new room filled with gifts, pausing to feel the warmth, to understand that it was real, and then came on.

When it was over, they lay on their backs, the cool desert air wafting through the open windows. The ceiling fan clacked above them.

"Boy, you had a lot in you," she said.

"You could tell?"

"Yes, I could tell."

She rolled toward him, studied his face. "So, tell me again, what are you doing here?"

He hesitated. "I told you. I came out to run my own business. They won't license another outfitter on the Chattooga."

"Why didn't you look somewhere else in the area? There are lots of rivers, right?"

"I just needed to get away from there."

"Why? Did something happen?"

Blood surged into his head. If he wanted to be close to this woman, he owed her an explanation.

An air horn sounded in the distance. He sat up. "Shit."

"What, the train?"

"Cover your ears. This is going to be loud."

He hopped out of bed and closed the windows.

The air began to vibrate. He held her close. BANG. The shock wave hit the windows, followed by the squelch and scream of steel wheels on rails. Carmen winced at the assault. On and on, it went, car after car. It pained him to see her cower.

Finally, the train passed, and so, too, did the magic of the night.

She took her hands from her ears. "God, how do you stand it?" she said.

"Actually, I've gotten used to it."

"I don't think I ever could. Not this close."

She gathered her clothes and rose from the bed.

"You're leaving?" he said.

"Yes. See you soon."

She kissed him on the forehead and disappeared down the stairs.

|Six|

Despite the regular appearance of the train, he and Carmen were now a couple. At first, they waited for the train to pass before they made love. But soon, they used the train to heighten the experience. He timed his penetration to the moment of the engine's passing and Carmen would cry out as the cars roared past. Afterward, they would laugh.

"Was that the loudest ever?"

"That was the loudest ever!"

After one of these lovemaking sessions, Carmen again asked if there was something he wasn't telling her. "I think you must be fleeing something," she said.

That was enough. He had to tell her something. "The truth is I got fired from my job," he said.

Her eyes went soft. "I'm sorry. What happened?"

"I hated my boss. I thought the way he ran the business was dangerous, sending us out on too many trips without enough rest. The Chattooga is a dangerous river."

"Did something happen?"

"No, but I don't want the guides out here to know I was fired. That's the kind of thing that gets spread around. I'm going to have enough trouble as it is getting this business off the ground."

"I see."

He could sense that she knew there was something more. But she didn't press him about it. That was one of the things he loved about Carmen. She knew when to let things lie.

As the summer progressed, their affection for each other grew. He asked her to move in with him. She said no. She wanted to maintain her home and office, both out of her desire for independence and for the practical purpose of taking care of resident animals. And she liked air conditioning. August temperatures rose above 100 degrees every day, shriveling plants, forcing people indoors until the sun went down.

In September, the heat finally broke. Ducharme proposed a Sunday hike into the mountains of the Big Bend National Park, where the air was cool and trees shaded the trail. Carmen readily agreed.

They arrived in the park on the tail end of a thunderstorm. Clouds fled the peaks of the Chisos Mountains and the sun burst through, turning the sotol grasslands electric green. He rolled down the window and steered the van up the switchbacked road, the temperature dropping at every turn. They pulled into the Lost Mine Trailhead, stepped out into cool, moist air.

"Estas listo, querida?" he said. Are you ready?

"Estoy listo."

They entered the forest, reveling in the lime green canopy of Gambel oak and the pungent smell of Pinyon pine. Following the rain, animals were out feeding. A pair of tiny Sierra del Carmen deer grazed above them, barely a stone's throw away. A bull snake, body checkered yellow and brown, slithered across the trail, followed by a

Mexican jay who snatched a juniper berry from in front of their feet. Ducharme hadn't seen this much wildlife in a month around Aintry.

They walked a mile up the ridgeline and stopped at an overlook. The flat-topped peak of Casa Grande rose in the near distance, further down the valley the giant tusk of Elephant Mountain, and to the west the twin spires of the Mules Ears. Where else in the world could you see these crazy forms, sprung from the depths of the earth?

They sat shoulder to shoulder on the soft grass. "I love this," Carmen said. "All the time I've lived in Aintry, I've never climbed this trail. It took a Georgia boy to bring me here."

He smiled, encouraged now to ask the question. "So, could you ever marry a Georgia boy?"

"Ever?"

"In the foreseeable future."

Carmen's eyes darkened. "Honestly, Robbie, I don't know if this venture of yours is going to fly. And if it doesn't, something tells me you'll want to leave Texas. And I'm not going to leave. This is my home, this is my family."

He stared into the valley, searching for the river behind the mountains. "I'll make it work."

***

In mid-November, after a period of extended rain, the Rio Grande rose to where it became runnable through the Big Bend. Ducharme received his first group of seven clients and led them on a successful trip of the Lower Canyons. The experience was everything he'd hoped for—great weather, great scenery, and an appreciative group. He led another trip in late November, equally as enjoyable as the first. Counting tips, he now had a respectable $35,000 in the bank.

To celebrate, he decided to bring Carmen lunch. He picked up some burritos and Mexican soda at the café and brought them over to her house. A customer's car stood in the driveway, so he went around back and entered through the door to the operating room. Carmen was standing with an older man that he'd seen at the post office—buzz cut and a pot belly. Probably retired military. The man cradled a miniature poodle in his arms. He nodded to Ducharme and went on with his conversation.

"She's not been eating like she used to. The other day I felt this knot in her back. She just about lives in my arms, so I knew right away something was different."

"Will you let me feel you, Precious?" Carmen said to the dog.

Precious growled.

"She's real protective when I'm around," the man said.

"Why don't you leave her?" Carmen said. "I'll let her settle in and then give her an examination. Let's put her in one of these pens."

The man carried her to the open cage and gave her a parting kiss. "You be good, Precious. I'll be back in a little bit."

He departed through the front door.

Ducharme lifted his armload of groceries. "I brought us some lunch."

"Great. Set in on the counter. Let me look at Precious first."

She opened the door to the pen and reached in. Precious growled, backed into a corner.

"O.K. Alright. I'll let you come to me."

Carmen took her hand away and stepped back. In an instant, the dog leapt through the cage door, sprinted under the operating table, and out the crack in the door at the back of the room.

Ducharme jumped up. "Oh, shit."

He opened the door and scanned the agave plants in the yard. Was she hiding beneath the leaves? He heard the hiss of the air brakes out by the highway. No. No way. When he arrived, the 18-wheeler stood idling on the side of the road. A hundred feet behind lay what looked like a piece of white shag carpet with blood pooling on one side.

"Oh, man!"

Carmen came up from behind. She covered her face with her hands.

"I'm really sorry, folks," the driver said.

Ducharme waved him off. "We'll take care of it."

The driver departed, leaving Ducharme alone with Carmen. He touched her shoulder. "I'm so sorry, babe."

She sat down by the side of the road, shaking her head.

"What do you want me to do?" he asked.

"Get a plastic bag. I've got some in the kitchen. And bring me a pair of gloves."

He ran to the house and came back with the items. A car had pulled over to the side of the road, the driver standing with Carmen. He looked familiar.

"I'd appreciate if you not talk to anyone about this," Carmen said to the man.

"Oh, no. I understand."

Carmen took the gloves and the bag. She walked out onto the pavement, put on the gloves and peeled Precious off the road. She dropped the poodle in the bag.

"Thanks for stopping," Ducharme said to the man. "We'll take it from here."

He followed her back to the house, waited in the front office until Carmen disposed of the dog. He heard her on her cellphone, speaking in a professional tone to a man who must have wanted her dead.

"It was my fault," he said when she got off the phone. "I forgot to shut the door."

She stared at him with pure disgust. "Do you know what this will do to my reputation, to my business?" she said. "I could be finished in this town. Not you, me."

"Is there anything I can do? Please tell me if there is."

"Leave," she said. "Just leave."

|Seven|

Janey woke to find herself spooned against the impossibly long body of her teenage daughter. The airport motel in Midland-Odessa had had only one room left, and that with a king. Surprisingly, Lara did not object. As much as her daughter might reject every other aspect of their being together, she could still show signs of dependency and affection.

Janey, however, had not slept well. Over the course of the night, she thought of everything that could go wrong on a five-day trip—broken ankle, snakebite, ruptured spleen. Surely, something would happen to someone.

When the alarm went off at 7, she felt she had just fallen asleep. She struggled to the bathroom, downed her regimen of drugs, and prodded her daughter awake.

"Come on, Lara, we've got the orientation meeting in an hour."

"I need to sleep."

"It's 8 o'clock our time. You need to get up."

Lara picked up her iPhone off the bedside table and started scrolling though her messages.

"Not now," Janey said.

"Just a minute. God!"

Lara's foul mood continued to the buffet breakfast.

"This food is disgusting," she said as she lifted the top off the scrambled eggs.

"You have to eat something," Janey said. "We're going to be canoeing today."

"I thought you said we were only *driving*?"

They were fifteen minutes late to the meeting in Robbie's room, and because the others had taken up the chairs and beds, they had to sit on the floor. There was only one other woman in the group. She looked to be about thirty, too old to be a companion for Lara. This was going to be hard on her.

Robbie Ducharme welcomed everyone and assured them they were in store for a wonderful time. He gave a brief introduction of himself as a guide of ten years' standing, formerly from Georgia and now living in some town called Aintry. He then asked everyone to introduce themselves and say what they hoped to get out of the trip.

Richard, who'd been writing notes on a pad, described himself as "one of the four realtors from Cary, North Carolina." He was dressed in worn REI gear, suggesting that he'd been in the outdoors before. In fact, he said that he'd rafted down the Rio Grande through the Big Bend National Park some years ago, that it had been spectacular, but the guide had said, "You ought to see the Lower Canyons."

"So, here I am," he said.

Parker Pierson had a perfect name for a realtor and the clothes to match. She wore salmon-colored chinos to go with her coiffed blonde hair. She surprised Janey by saying she was "looking to add some brightness in her life" after the death of her mother. Janey appreciated her having been through recent suffering and thought maybe they could bond on this trip.

Archie was apparently the joker of the group, loudly announcing that he had "no idea why he was here," but that he was "hoping to have some fun." He wore a yellow Ralph Lauren Polo shirt and khakis that were surely not going in his river duffel. He reminded her of one of Worth's nicer friends and she looked forward to a little levity on the trip.

The fourth realtor introduced himself as "Peter Bayer," to which Archie interjected, "We call him 'Pooh Bear.'" He was a pudgy man with a small mouth and short white hair that stood up on his head. He said he was looking forward to seeing some new sights and a chance to be with friends. Presumably, he'd put up with Archie's jibes before.

Janey went next. She described her job as an admissions counselor at Georgia Tech in Atlanta. She said she was the mother of two wonderful girls. She spoke about her desire to take on new challenges after a difficult period in her life. "And I'm hoping to have an adventure with my daughter."

Lara, who was staring at her phone, missed the comment. But she did notice the silence that followed. She looked up. "My turn? O.K., my name is Lara. I'm a sophomore in high school. I really don't know much about this trip, but my mom thought it would be a good idea. I like hiking and canoeing, so…"

She'd hoped Lara would say something about bonding with her mother, but that would have been too much of a concession. At least she put her phone down.

The last to speak was the epitome of tall, dark, and handsome. He'd been sitting on a chair in the corner, showing little reaction to any of the introductions. His name was Janko. He said he was from Chicago, but spoke with a strong Slavic accent.

"Is that 'Dagick' or 'Dagich'?" Robbie asked.

"'Dagich.' Like an itch."

He had small ears and short hair that came to a spade-shaped point at the top of his forehead.

"I'm interested in experiencing this wilderness," he said. "In Europe, you can't roll a boulder off a cliff without getting arrested."

Janey thought this a curious statement. Who cared about rolling boulders off of cliffs? It was certainly not why she'd come, but everyone had their reasons.

Robbie then described the unique nature of the Big Bend. He held up a map of West Texas, pointing out where the Rio Grande made a giant U-turn, flowing southeast and then northeast.

"All of this area was once under a warm, shallow sea," he said. "As sea creatures died and their bones and shells settled into the mud, they were compressed into limestone, forming the walls of the canyons through which the Rio Grande now flows. We'll see some of these fossils as we go down the river."

He went on about the collision of continental plates that formed the Rocky Mountains, of which the Big Bend was the southern end, and the volcanic eruptions that followed. "You'll see old cindercones and lava fields as we drive down through the park. I can see one right outside my window in Aintry."

She wondered about Ducharme's home life. Was he married? There was no ring on his left hand. Curiously, he was missing the top half of his right pinkie finger. What was the story with that?

"When all this mountain building ended, the forces of nature began tearing it down. Rainfall dissolved the limestone. Plants rooted in cracks, split the rock and sent it tumbling down to the valleys. The Rio Grande took shape, forcing its way through the mountains all the way to the Gulf of Mexico. As the philosopher Heraclitus once said, there is nothing permanent except change."

Well, listen to him! Janey thought. This man was clearly well-read. She found that attractive, but wondered why someone with his education was leading one-man trips through the wilderness. Where were his assistants? Was he going to cook and clean, as well as guide?

His geology lesson over, Ducharme went on to talk about the human history of the region. There was some early tribe of Indians called the Jumanos, who were pushed out by the Apaches, who had been pushed south from the plains by the Comanches. The Spanish arrived in the 1500s, building missions and forts to protect the missions. But the Apaches raided them constantly, stealing livestock and killing men, women and children. Not many people wanted to live in the area, which prompted the Mexican government to encourage Americans to settle there.

"And we all know how that worked out," Ducharme said. "The residents of this area grew embittered from what they saw as a lack of support from the central government. In 1844, they launched a war of independence from Mexico, declaring themselves a Republic of Texas. When the Mexican government objected, the American government declared war on them and eventually came away with 500,000 square miles of Mexican land, including what is now the states of Texas,

California, Nevada, Utah and Arizona. Pretty good deal, huh?"

"Remember the Alamo!" Richard chimed in.

That got Janko's attention. He seemed not to like this mockery of American territorial ambition.

Robbie just smiled. "Now, let's talk about the section of river we're going to be running," he said. "Most commercial trips focus on the stretch of river that borders the Big Bend National Park. That's almost all flat water and a lot of it is through desert. We're going to be running the section immediately downstream of the park—the Lower Canyons. It goes through the some of the most amazing rock formations you'll ever see, and there will be plenty of whitewater."

He went on to say that this stretch of river had a dozen "named" rapids and many more that required skill to get through.

"You've all indicated that you have whitewater experience, and you will be put to the test," he said.

Those words of warning put Janey on edge. She'd read the description of the trip in Robbie's letter, but she hadn't really absorbed all this about the rapids. What if she tipped over repeatedly, got injured, or too afraid to go on?

"We'll be hemmed in by canyons most of the way, surrounded by the most inhospitable desert landscape in the country," Robbie said. "Once we start down the river, there's no getting off."

"Is there phone service?" Lara asked.

"Not once we get in the canyons. And I urge you all to leave your phones here at the motel. The staff said we could put suitcases in their storage closet until we return."

Lara showed no reaction to that, but Janey could

imagine what she was thinking. This is the end of the world.

Robbie went on to talk about rattlesnakes and tarantulas and a pig-like animal called a javelina with razor-sharp tusks. Then, he talked about all the cactus and how the thorns could stick you and were difficult to pull out. She found herself growing angry at Robbie for scaring everyone, and angry at herself for not having researched this trip more carefully.

"Pooh Bear wants to know if there are mountain lions," Archie said, poking his friend.

"There are mountain lions, but you won't see them," Robbie said. "They may be watching you from up on the canyon walls, but you will not see them."

"Will we see other people on the river?" Richard asked.

"Probably not. There are other outfitters and private boaters that run the Lower Canyons, but not many. We'll very likely be alone the whole six days."

Parker asked what they should wear on the river.

"If you're prone to sunburn, I recommend you wear long pants and a long-sleeved shirt. You definitely want to wear a hat. If you don't paddle all the time, I recommend gloves so you don't get blisters."

Gloves, Janey thought. He didn't say anything about gloves in the letter.

"I've got a backpacking guitar," Richard said. "Can I bring that?"

"If you can fit it in your canoe, you can bring it."

Seeing there were no more questions, he handed everyone a waterproof duffel bag. "Put your clothes and your sleeping bags in these bags," he said. "I've got tents in a separate bag and will hand those out on the river."

Janey frowned. "You said we should bring our own tents if we wanted. I went to a lot of trouble to bring ours."

"I said that?"

"Yes, it was in your letter," Janey said.

Robbie winced. "That was my policy on the first trip, but some people brought oversized tents that didn't pack well, so I bought my own. I guess I forgot to mention that in the letter. Just leave yours in the van, Janey."

She shook her head.

"I need you to have everything packed up and out by the van by check out time at 11," he said. "We have a four-hour drive ahead of us and then a couple mile paddle to our campsite."

Everyone got up to leave. She lingered in the room.

"Mom, are you coming?" Lara said.

"I'll be there in a minute."

***

In the parking lot, Robbie collected the duffel bags and strapped them down in the canoe trailer next to Rubbermaid containers full of food and cooking supplies.

Richard, Parker and Archie graciously climbed in the back seat of the van. Janey and Lara sat in the middle seat, while Janko and Pooh Bear remained outside. It was apparent that each one of them wanted the front seat. Pooh Bear went back to the trailer and said something to Robbie.

"Go ahead and sit in front, then," Robbie answered.

Hearing Robbie's response, Janko got in the middle seat next to Lara.

Robbie got in the driver's seat and closed the door. A

sickly smell of cologne filled the van.

"Is everybody good?" Robbie asked.

"Can we have some air back here?" Janey said. "Someone went a little overboard on the aftershave."

"That's Pooh Bear," Archie said. "He can't get enough of Old Spice."

Pooh Bear mumbled apologies. Robbie turned on the air conditioning, and they were off.

The landscape south of Midland-Odessa was a dreary patchwork of scrub brush and oil wells. She had been told the Big Bend had the most spectacular scenery in Texas, but this was anything but. Eventually, the passengers in the back seat fell asleep, their snoring rising above the hum of the tires. Sitting next to Lara, Janko said nothing, just stared out the window. Janey decided to break the ice.

"Are you from Eastern Europe?" she asked.

He fixed her with his dark eyes. "Croatia."

"Lots of good tennis players from there."

"Tennis players and beautiful women."

She let that slide.

"And you are from Atlanta," he said.

"Yes."

He looked at Lara. "Are you an only child?"

"No," she said. "I have an older sister."

"She was not invited?"

"She was, but..." She glanced at her mother. "She's kind of moving in with my dad."

Great. Her single status was now on the table.

"You're very brave to come with all these men," he said.

She rolled her eyes. "*Yea*-uh. One of many things I wasn't told about this trip."

Janko winked at Janey.

The dreary landscape continued, scrub and more scrub. At Fort Stockton, they stopped for lunch at a fast food restaurant. Robbie topped off the gas and they headed south through Marathon and on toward the Big Bend National Park. The landscape grew more interesting with low mountain ranges shaped like layered slabs— "flatirons" Robbie called them.

He raised his voice. "Folks, we are traveling along what was once called 'The Comanche Trail.' The Comanches lived up in the Great Plains, but once a year during what was called 'The Comanche Moon,' they would ride horses and travel south all the way to Mexico. This area was dominated by the Apaches, but the Comanches would march right through and raid the Spanish settlements across the river, take cattle and prisoners and force them to march back north. They say the thoroughfare created by this march was more than a mile wide in places."

"What happened to the Indians?" Archie said.

"The Apaches were still raiding settlements in Mexico and Texas on into the late 1800s," Ducharme said. "As late as the 1880s, the Mexican government was paying Americans for Apache scalps."

"One bounty hunter claimed to have taken 487," Richard said.

Lara blanched. "White people scalped Indians? That's gross!"

Janko glanced at Lara with an amused expression. This was not news to him.

Finally, they entered the Big Bend National Park and stopped at the Visitor's Center to get a permit to run the river.

"This will be your last chance for six days to use a regular toilet," Robbie said. "Otherwise, you'll be using my Honey Pot."

Janey's innards were still in turmoil. She savored her last visit to the women's room, only to come out to the parking lot to find Lara looking at her phone.

"I thought you were going to leave that at the motel?" she said.

"He said we *could* leave them at the motel. He didn't say we had to."

"That's not what I heard."

Vowing not to carry this any further, she boarded and focused on the world outside. The mountains were getting very interesting—flat-topped, cones, jagged peaks—not all the same like most ranges she'd seen. But there was no sign of water anywhere—no creeks or ponds. They started down a gradual decline, slowed, and bounced to a halt in a dirt track. There between a pair of gravel bars, was a muddy little river.

"Folks, this is it," Robbie said. "The Rio Grande."

Lara stepped out and looked at her phone. "Great. No service."

|Eight|

The first thing Gallagher did after being awoken by the sheriff was drive to the bank and cash his $2,000 check.

"Make that ten twenties and the rest in hundreds," he said to the young teller.

"Did you just win the lottery?" she asked.

"No, sweetie, I just got fired."

He had breakfast at the Fort Davis Drug Store, then headed south on Highway 166. For the past year, he'd seen an Airstream trailer with a For Sale sign on it parked in front of a house outside of Valentine. He could write the script in his head—couple retires from the ranching life, buys a trailer and travels the state for a few years. Then, one of them has a stroke or gets the cancer and the roving life is over. The trailer goes up for sale.

He pulled in the drive. The house was old timey adobe with cedar posts holding up the front porch. He counted three layers of roofing, tin being the last. He knocked on the door and a suitably decrepit man answered. He'd be six feet tall if he could straighten his knees. Bent as he was, he was maybe five eight.

"Danny Gallagher out of Fort Davis. I've passed by your trailer here many a time and thought I might have a look."

The man nodded. "I'll get you the key. Forgive me if I don't join you. My knees are about shot, as you can see."

Gallagher smelled mouse shit as soon as he opened the door. These trailers might be as tight as a bank vault, but you can't keep out a determined mouse. The "wood grain" walls were a plastic laminate. He opened one of the cabinets. Hardware was still good. The control center over the sink bed looked OK, as did the bed and toilet.

He went outside and studied the rolled up awning over the door. The hardware had rusted out. And the tires definitely needed replacing. Hopefully, she'd still roll. He went back to the house and knocked on the door.

"What are you asking?"

"I'll take $5,000. That's nothing compared to what I paid for it new."

"When was that?"

The man looked at the floor, put his hand to his forehead. "I don't know. It was back when we both retired. My wife would remember, but she's been gone a year."

"It's tough being alone, ain't it?" Gallagher said. He patted his shirt pocket, pulled out a cigarette. He lit it, turned around, and pretended to study the trailer.

"Those tires need replacing. Awning hardware, too. You've got mice inside. I'll give you $1,000 cash."

The man shook his head. "I can't let it go for that."

Gallagher drew on his cigarette. "How many years are you going to let it sit out there?"

"I don't know. It's been out there awhile."

"Let me see your hand."

He reached in his pocket and laid ten hundred dollar bills in the man's palm. "How does that feel?"

The man weighed the money. "Another five would feel

about right."

He peeled off five more hundreds. "You've got a deal."

Gallagher hitched the Airstream to his pickup and drove it out to the highway, stopping to make sure the tires were holding air. The F150 balked at the load, but by the time he got it up to 60, everything rolled smoothly along.

Just outside of Valentine, he passed the phony Prada store some artist out of Marfa had built by the roadside. He didn't know what it was supposed to mean, but suspected it was a dig at locals like him. A carload of tourists were standing out front taking pictures. As he sped past, he blew his horn and gave them the finger.

In Marfa, he went to Dave's Gun Store and bought four boxes of ammunition for his pistol. "And I'll take one of those American flags," he said, pointing to the banner hanging on the wall behind the counter.

Next stop was The Get Go where he bought a week's worth of groceries and a case of PBR. He picked up a copy of the *Big Bend News* and gassed up the generator in the trailer. With that, he was off to the Rio Grande.

South of Marfa, the land lay barren save for a scattering of dagger plants standing out in the plain. A herd of Pronghorn antelope clustered by the highway, nibbling the sparse grass under the barbed wire fence. Pronghorns were rumored to have the sharpest eyesight in the animal kingdom. Just for fun, he slowed down, lowered the passenger side window and aimed his pistol at the biggest buck. The animal startled and burst away on stiff legs.

"Just kidding," he laughed.

The sky to the south grew dark with the promise of an afternoon thundershower. He looked forward to the cooler temperatures and the break in the relentless sunshine. What little greenery there was in this godforsaken landscape would brighten with the rain.

His mood soured as he entered Presidio, a sprawling collection of adobe and cinderblock homes on the Mexican border. There was not a blade of grass or a tree anywhere in sight. Every person in the street looked Hispanic. He stopped in a Quick Mart for a Coke. All the patrons were speaking Spanish.

"How ya' doin' today?" he said to the clerk.

"Fine, sir."

These chili chokers could speak English when they wanted.

The thunderstorm broke as he climbed back in the truck. The rain came hard, threatened to turn to hail.

"Don't you dent my new trailer," he said to the sky. "And don't put no stars in my windshield."

Fifteen minutes later, the storm had passed. He cranked down the window and inhaled the turpentine aroma of the creosote bushes. He crested a rise and the Rio Grande appeared right below him, running pretty as you please between a green band of river cane and honey mesquite trees. Up, down, up, down, the road rose and fell over the dry washes coming down from the hills. A wooden sign beside the road announced the entrance to the Big Bend Ranch State Park, neighbor to the Big Bend National Park. He turned into the entrance and approached the campsites. Just as he'd hoped, he had the whole place to himself. Tourists couldn't stand the summer's hundred-degree heat, but old Danny didn't mind. Like a rattlesnake in a cave, he'd hibernate during the day in his air-conditioned trailer, coming out when the sun went down.

He pulled into a spot at the outside of the loop, stepped out and stretched. To his right, a pair of twenty-foot-tall hoodoos loomed like space aliens. Hoodoos were pillars of rock eroded into weird shapes due to the different consistencies of the minerals at different strata. A hard upper layer resembling a head might remain atop an eroded "neck" and a wide "body."

Gallagher looked down on an olive green river no more than fifty feet wide, speckled white where it chattered over a small rapid. A man could wade across that and not get his knees wet. He lowered the awning on the trailer, retrieved his lawn chair and a six-pack of beer and settled in for the evening.

"Yes, siree, this is what I'm talking about," he said as he popped the top off the first beer. "You can kick Danny out, but you can't knock him down."

For the next month, he basked shirtless in his riverside home, watching roadrunners chase bugs through the underbrush, shooting scorpions with his pistol. A family of javelina moved beneath his trailer. He would feed them apple cores and sing to them, "*Have you seen the little piggies with their piggy eyes...*"

Unless it was absolutely necessary, he didn't bother to use the toilet in the trailer. Why bother wasting water? Instead, he pissed and shat in the river.

One morning in late September, he was doing his business when a shout came from upriver. He turned around to see a flotilla of canoes, the first of the season. The lettering on the side identified them as Big Bend Adventures out of Terlingua.

"Man, use a friggin' toilet!" the guide shouted.

Gallagher pointed to his rear end. "Kiss my ass, faggot!"

The guide scowled as he and the horrified guests went past. "Fuck you, too."

The boaters' appearance signaled the end of Gallagher's blissful isolation. The park rangers had been kind enough to let him stay at the same site beyond the two week maximum, but they would not do so much longer. At a minimum, he would have to change campgrounds.

The next evening, he packed up the trailer and headed east along the river. Nothing looked as appealing as the Hoodoos Campground and, before he knew it, he was in Terlingua, the one-time ghost town turned tourist trap and guide hangout. He parked in front of the Starlight Theater, taking three spots, buttoned his shirt and strolled inside.

The place was hopping this Saturday night with tourists, cowboys, and assorted outcasts. A grey-haired couple stood at the mike singing passable cowboy songs. Tattooed waitresses bustled between the tables. He took a seat at the bar and ordered a margarita.

"House tequila?" the bartender asked.

"If I have to."

He was two drinks in when a vaguely familiar face appeared beside him. Like neighborhood dogs, they sniffed each other out.

"Aren't you the guy who was shitting in the river?" the man said.

Gallagher stared at the river guide. "What of it?" he said. "A man's got a right to shit where he wants."

"You're disgusting, man. I could have you thrown out

of the park."

"You couldn't throw your whoring mother out of the park."

In a flash, they went at each other. Gallagher reached for the man's throat. The guide threw a right hand, knocking him backward off the stool. He remembered hitting his head on the floor, the ceiling starting to spin.

The next thing Gallagher knew, he was looking in the face of an EMT.

"Sir, can you tell me how many fingers I'm holding up?"

He counted three.

"Can you tell me your name?"

"Danny Gallager."

"Mr. Gallagher, you've had a mild concussion. Do you know where you are?"

He sat up to find a roomful of bar patrons staring at him.

"I know where I am."

"Do you have somewhere to stay?"

"I got my trailer out front."

"I suggest you find a place to park it and get a good night's sleep."

|Nine|

The city of San Pedro Sula was known as the most violent city in the most violent country in the world, Honduras. Rivera Hernandez, with its rampant gang culture and poverty, was San Pedro Sula's most violent neighborhood. Yet life went on. People strolled among tables of beautifully stacked produce in the open-air market. Children went to school. And every evening, teenagers gathered for pick-up soccer matches at the Parque Rivera Hernandez.

Sayda Pacheco, 15, was the only girl allowed to play in the 5 o'clock match. Her ball handling skills were the equal of any of the boys. She was stronger and faster than her twin brother, Kelin. Sayda, "the lucky one," and Kelin, "the slender one," were fraternal twins, but complications during pregnancy caused the former to receive most of her mother's nutrients, while the boy fetus suffered. Since the moment of her birth, Sayda had outshone her brother.

But Sayda's accomplishments did not come easily. On this day at the soccer field, she was being guarded by Oscar, one of the bigger boys. Every time someone would pass Sayda the ball, he would body up to her, knocking her off balance with his big chest. There was no referee to call fouls and her own protestations were ignored. The best she could do was to pass the ball off to someone else.

With the match tied 4–4 and time running out, she went over and whispered something to Kelin. He nodded and went back to his position as a midfielder and Sayda as a wing. When the ball next came to Kelin, he faked a pass to Sayda. Oscar closed in, ready to bump her off the ball. Instead, she spun around and raced downfield.

"Mira! Mira!" she called.

Kelin fired the ball ahead to her. She took the pass, dribbled downfield, and shot the ball passed the goalie. Game over.

Bystanders watching along the graffiti-covered stucco wall offered congratulations.

"Que golazo, Sayda!"

"Usted lo mostro!"

But her celebration was short lived. At the end of the field, a group of shirtless men, foreheads tattooed with the Roman numerals XIII, stood waiting. They were gang members of Mara Salvatrucha, MS 13. Sayda veered away, lingering against the far wall. But Kelin was not so lucky. The gang approached him, as they had done several times before, looming over the skinny boy. Sayda knew what they wanted and she could only hope that Kelin would refuse. He had been warned by his parents never to come home if he joined MS 13 or any other gang. He had no desire to join and told the gang members so.

"No soy un luchador," he said. I am not a fighter.

But this time, one of the members took hold of the boy and pointed towards Sayda. They knew how much he loved his sister, how he valued her protection. Now, she feared she was being made a bargaining chip.

When the gang members left, Sayda hurried to catch

up to Kelin. He was walking towards home, his hands covering his eyes. She could see he was crying.

"What did they say to you?" she asked.

"Don't talk to me," he said.

"You've got to tell me, Kelin. I know they were saying something about me."

He turned to her with desperate eyes. "They said if I didn't join the gang, they would rape you. All of them. They meant it."

Fear rushed to Sayda's head. "We have to tell our parents," she said.

"No, they said not to!"

"Kelin, we have to. We need their help!"

That night at dinner, they told their parents, Javier and Angely, about the gang's latest threat. Angely's face went white. She looked to her husband.

"We have to get them out," she said. "It's time."

Javier held his head in his hand.

"I might as well tell you, they've threatened your father, too," Angely said. "They say he must pay a 'war tax' if he wants to keep the shop open."

"What did you tell them, Papa?" Sayda said.

"I got my shotgun out and chased them from the store," he said.

Kelin began to cry. "They're going to kill me. I know it."

Angely put her arm around her son. "Call your friend in Texas," she said to Javier. "Tell him we're sending the children his way."

Javier nodded, his bushy eyebrows knit together. "I'll do it. I'll call him tonight."

The next evening, the family gathered in their living

room with the orange painted stucco walls and the framed portrait of the Virgin of Guadalupe. Their uncle in Texas agreed to take Sayda and Kelin, but only under one condition—that they receive asylum from the U.S. government. Undocumented immigrants were being swept up and sent back in droves, and their uncle didn't want to risk his own jailing or deportation if he was caught sheltering illegals.

"He told me it has become impossible to gain asylum just by claiming you have been threatened by gang violence," Javier said. "You must have proof."

"You must write a letter," Angeley said to Javier.

"Jorge said that's unlikely to work," Javier said. "It has to be from some official source—a police document or a newspaper article."

"What about the cost?" Sayda said.

Her father shook his head. "He said to be prepared to pay $8,000 for each of you. Most of it goes to smugglers."

Angeley wailed, "Oh, my God, we'll have to sell everything!"

"Can't we do it on our own?" Sayda said.

Javier shook his head. "You'd just get caught and sent back. I've heard this many times."

In the coming days, the family gathered information on possible routes to the U.S. The Mexican government had cracked down on Central American immigrants traveling north through its southern states, so even that part of the trip was no longer easy. Riding atop trains had become almost impossible due to regular police sweeps of the railyards and trains. Buses were a possible mode, but the police made regular checks of passengers, especially children. If they couldn't show legal entry or couldn't pay bribes, they would be sent back to their home countries. Even if you could make it to the U.S. border, crossing had become exceedingly difficult. Long sections of wall had been built in all the major cities along the border. Cameras and drones watched for swimmers and climbers. Legal border crossings were equipped with high tech sensors that could detect bodies hidden beneath seats or inside trailers. Only in the remotest areas was it possible to cross with ease, and that meant days of trekking though arid deserts on both sides of the border.

The following week, Sayda and Kelin gathered at El Parque de Riviera Hernandez for the 5 o' clock pick-up soccer match. She surveyed the crowd gathered around the edges. There was no sign of MS 13. The whistle blew and she sprung into action. She was running down the right sideline when someone threw something over the wall in front of her. At first, she thought it was another soccer ball and prepared to kick it off the field. But as it rolled to a halt, she saw that it was not a ball. It had hair on top, and eyes and lips. It was a face—the face of her father.

***

The following day, family and friends gathered at the Pacheco home. Kelin burrowed in his mother's arms. His grandfather tried to console him.

"Don't worry, Kelin," his grandmother said. "We will protect you."

"Solo quiero vivir," he moaned. I just want to live.

The guests pledged money to help him and Sayda flee to the north. Angeley gratefully accepted their money. But there was still the fear that the children would be caught somewhere along the way and returned. No one wanted to think of what fate might await them in that instance.

Then, the children's grandfather appeared with a newspaper tucked under his arm. He laid it on the table, open to a short article with a headline that read, "Shopkeeper Beheaded."

Boney finger shaking, he pointed to the article and said to Angeley, "This is it. Your childrens' ticket to asylum."

|Ten|

All the equipment for Ducharme's trip—the cooking gear, the tents, the food, the jugs of water—lay spread out on the gravel bar beside the Rio Grande. He checked and rechecked every item. Last time, he'd forgotten the juice boxes and the clients had only water to drink for six days. Finally, he was satisfied that everything was present. He announced the boat assignments—Parker with him, Janey with Lara, Peter with Archie, and Janko with Richard.

Paddling assignments were a tricky business. Two people paddling a canoe was not like six people paddling a raft. In a raft, a guide did most of the steering, and a weak paddler didn't significantly slow things down. In a canoe, the responsibility for keeping the boat straight, for maneuvering through rapids and propelling through flatwater rested with just two people. The situation was rife for conflict. Who was responsible for hitting that last rock? Why can't you keep the boat straight? Ducharme only took people with canoeing experience on the Lower Canyons, but there was always potential for conflict.

In making boat assignments, he started out with the obvious pairings—husbands with wives, parent with child. But over time, he liked to mix things up, to try out new combinations. It was a good way to avoid anyone feeling stuck with a certain partner. And it was a good way for people to get to know each other.

The assignments made, he instructed everyone how to load their gear. "Jerry cans go under the center thwart, your waterproof duffel bags to either side of the thwart. In addition to your own stuff, I'm going to give each of you a communal gear bag. It may have tents in it, or cooking gear, or the Honey Pot. Whatever I give you stays with the boat for the whole trip."

He gave each boat an extra paddle and a throw rope to be used for rescuing swimmers. Before setting off, he instructed everyone to blow up the air bags clipped into the bow and stern. These would help keep the canoes afloat if they were to tip over.

By the time these sixteen-foot-long canoes were loaded, they weighed more than 170 pounds each. It took maximum strength to lift them the few yards from the gravel bar to floatable water.

"God, I can't believe I'm going to paddle this thing for six days," Archie said.

Ducharme smiled. "You'll get used to it."

As a last preparation, he took out the clear plastic pouch holding the topographic maps of the Lower Canyons. On the maps, the Rio Grande appeared as a blue ribbon, bordered on each side by brown lines demarcating forty foot changes in elevation. Where the river ran through the canyons, as many as a dozen lines ran so close together as to become blurred. In the coming days, as they went deeper into the canyons, the number of lines would double.

"Archie, you and Peter paddle sweep," he said referring to the boat in the last position. "We'll trade off each day."

"Did you hear that, Pooh Bear?" Archie said. "No paddling ahead of everyone else."

With that, Ducharme pushed off the bottom. A dozen hard strokes and he and Parker had the canoe up to speed. He loved that first feeling of gliding across the surface, the air against his face. He loved looking out on all the equipment packed into the long, narrow hull. Aside from people, and enough money to run the business, this was all he needed in life.

The Rio Grande was finally up and moving, flush with the rains of November. It carried a heavy load of silt clawed from the barren expanse of West Texas and southern New Mexico. But these muddy waters would be enough to carry him and his clients away from whatever boring or troubling thoughts plagued them in their city lives and deliver them to a state of wonder, the wonder of the Lower Canyons.

As with most late fall days in the Big Bend, this one was cloudless and windless. He glanced behind. The canoes were all in a line spaced by a dozen or so yards. This seemed like a good group. He felt reasonably confident he could get along with everyone, with the possible exception of Janey Hart.

After the orientation meeting in the motel, Janey had accosted him, her bird-like face contorted in anger. She said he had underplayed the hazards of the trip in his letter and that she might not have signed up if she'd known about all the rapids. He assured her that she would be fine, that he would paddle her canoe through any rapids she did not feel comfortable with. She then asked why he needed to know an applicant's marital status. He apologized and explained that he'd simply copied the form from a company he used to work for. He said he would eliminate that question in the future. Finally, she complained that other members appeared to have paddling gloves, but those had not been listed among the necessary clothing items and so she did not bring any. Fortunately, he had an extra pair of gloves in his duffel bag. He dug those out and presented them to her, which seemed to mollify her somewhat.

Was Janey just nervous about the trip, or was she thin-skinned? The latter might explain her apparently single status. A constant complainer could make things unpleasant for all the members of the trip. He'd had his share of those on the Chattooga.

As he paddled, he ran through a mental roster of his clients. He still used the word association trick from his High Five days to remember first names. For this crew, Archie was Archie the Comic, Janey was Jane the Pain. There was Lara with the blonde Hairah, Richard the Professor, and Pooh Bear Peter. Only Janko defied easy word association. He decided to go with his last name, Dagic, the Man with the Itch. It wasn't a perfect match. The man seemed calm on the outside, but something about the way he eyed his tripmates in the motel room made Ducharme think he was sizing up their relative strengths and weaknesses. Soon, he had a feeling, Dagic would establish his presence as first among the clients.

He glanced over his shoulder. Sure enough, Dagic and Richard had moved into position behind him. Dagic had a respectable J-stroke, the twist of the paddle at the end of each stroke that helped keep the canoe straight. Archie and Peter came next, Archie chattering away non-stop. Janey and Lara picked up the rear. Lara's stroke looked weak, or rather she wasn't trying. Eyes unfocused, her face was a mask of disdain. He would have thought that ironic given the incredible surroundings, but he'd seen it with teenaged clients before. They were in their own world, waging some inner battle.

The plan for this first afternoon was to canoe just six miles, enough time for people to break in their strokes, but not get exhausted. The river here was easy—the hundred-foot-wide channel shallow and slow.

A mile along, the first canyon appeared. Heath was one of the smallest of the Lower Canyons, but to anyone who'd never canoed in the West, it was like entering the gates to paradise. Above the reedy waterline, talus—rocks and boulders that had fallen from the cliffs—created a slope about one hundred feet high. Grass grew on these slopes giving the false impression that they were easy to climb. They were not, as the loose rock and intermittent cactus defeated efforts to gain footing.

Above the talus, sheer cliffs rose another three hundred feet. Rainwater had eroded the limestone over the millennia, creating vertical grooves, crenellations and circular mouths—bocas—that gave the cliffs definition.

"Folks, we're about to enter Heath Canyon," he said. "This is just the first of many."

Parker craned her head. "Oh, this is just stunning!"

"All of this is made up of layers of limestone, which means all of it was underwater at some time," he said. "Limestone is made of the shells of sea creatures that sank and were compressed in bottom mud. They say it takes a thousand years of deposition to create one inch of rock, so when we pass through these thousand-foot-high canyons, think of how old that rock is."

Janey called from behind. "There's some kind of falcon. It just landed near the top."

He turned and followed her gaze.

"I think it's an Aplomado Falcon!" she said.

He'd not seen the bird and doubted she could correctly identify it. There were a lot of falcons in the Lower Canyons. He lifted his binoculars and scanned the cliffside. There it was. A black-and-white striped head and a black and orange belly.

"You call that an Aplomado Falcon?" he said.

"Yes."

"I take it you're a birder."

"Yes, I am," she said.

So she was more than just a complainer.

A mile beyond Heath Canyon, he directed the canoeists to shore on the Mexican side. Here, he said, they would take a short walk through the lowlands to see the different kinds of cactus.

"There's a saying that everything that grows in the Chihuahuan Desert is designed to prick, poke, or sting, so be careful where you put your feet."

Within minutes, he'd identified a dozen different species. There was the prickly pear whose flat green lobes were speckled with purple aereoles, each one bristling with half-a-dozen spines. The wright fishhook was no bigger than a grapefruit, but had hooked spines four inches long. The horse crippler was shaped like a cow paddy, flat and circular, cross-hatched with heavy spines that could pierce the flesh of unwary livestock. Janey knelt down to photograph them with a DSLR camera. Richard took notes. Archie, predictably, went for laughs.

"Robbie, which would be the worst one to be shoved onto?" he said.

"I haven't sampled each of them, but that would probably be the prickly pear," he said. "The spines would stab you. On top of that, they have these little hairs called glochids that stick in your flesh. The glochids have barbed ends and when you try to pull them out, the ends break off. I brushed against one of those a few months ago and it itched for a week."

While the others hesitated in walking through the brush, Dagic moved with ease, turning sideways to fit through the narrowest of openings. He'd clearly been in the outdoors before.

He scuffed at the hard dirt, reached over to finger the powdery surface. "What is this?" he said.

"It's called caliche," Ducharme said. "It's like a natural cement. Binds together sand and clay. It's almost impossible to dig through."

"Hard to bury a man in this."

He let that pass, but when Dagic started prodding a prickly pear with his boot, Ducharme spoke up. "I wouldn't do that. Those spines will go right through leather."

Dagic gave him a smile. "Good to know."

"O.K., let's move on. We've got three miles to the campsite."

They loaded back into their canoes and headed downstream.

The campsite stood on the Mexican side of the river, on a riverside bluff beneath a thousand-foot wall of the Sierrita de Guadelupe. Landing onshore, he instructed Dagic and Richard to empty their canoe and bring it up to flat ground. There, he showed them how to turn it over and level it with rocks. This would serve as his "kitchen counter" on which to put the stove, pots, and utensils. He instructed Janey and Lara to bring their canoe nearby and turn it over to serve as a "couch" for people to sit against.

Once this was done, he instructed everyone to pair up with a sleeping partner, grab a tent out of the tent bag, and find a level site. "Parker, you have a tent to yourself. Janko, you are in a tent with me, but I like to sleep in my canoe so you have it to yourself unless in rains."

He pulled a tent out to give to Dagic.

"I think I'll sleep out, too," Dagic said. "I like to see who's coming."

He smiled. "This isn't *Deliverance*. There's no one out here but coyotes and javelina."

"Just the same."

He put the tent back in the bag. "If you're not putting up a tent, would you mind setting up the Honey Bucket? I'll show you how."

He got out the portable toilet and went through the steps of fitting a plastic bag in the bucket and then pouring in a layer of sawdust. The sawdust bag was to be left beside the Honey Pot so users could add another layer after they did their business.

"Put this someplace out of the way, but make sure there's a clear path to it. We don't want anyone stepping on a cactus in the middle of the night."

"Yah, sure."

While Dagic went off to set up the bathroom, Ducharme fired up the twin burner gas stove and started dinner preparations. He could hear the click of the aluminum poles and the varied conversations as his clients tried to figure out how to erect their tents. Janey and Lara disagreed as to which sleeve the first pole went into. They stood it up one way, didn't like it, stood it up another. Finally, they got it right and disappeared inside.

Janey was the first to reemerge. She was dressed in tights and a V-neck T-shirt, her ash blonde hair pulled back with a band. She ambled to the kitchen.

"What are you making us tonight?" she said.

"I call it the Texas Two-Step," he said. "Red beans and rice, corn, diced tomatoes and chili peppers served with pita bread."

"Can I help?"

"Thank you, no. I've got it under control."

"Wow, a man who works and cooks."

It was nice to see her smile for a change. She was obviously more comfortable on shore.

"How are those gloves working out?" he said.

"They're great. I don't think I'll have any trouble."

"You look like you can handle the stern pretty well. Did you learn that J-stroke in summer camp?"

"Yes. A long time ago."

He pictured her as a girl, no wrinkle lines around her mouth, the little belly absent. She must have been a real fox.

When the rice was done, he added in the other ingredients. The rest of the crew began to filter in to the kitchen area.

"There's beer in the cooler," he said. "Enough for two apiece. Drink it up tonight, because the ice will be melted by tomorrow."

They picked out their beers and leaned back against the canoe couches. Talk arose around the first day's paddling.

"Pooh Bear wanted to visit the reeds," Archie said. "I kept telling him it wasn't time to eat yet."

Parker laughed. "I had it easy. Robbie did most of the paddling and all the steering."

Richard busied himself writing notes. Peter peered over his shoulder.

"What are you doing? Writing a novel?"

"I'm keeping a trip diary," Richard said.

"Richard's writing a tell-all," Archie said. "You all better watch yourselves."

Lara appeared in the shortest of shorts. Everyone turned to watch as she approached, her long, tan legs like a pair of exclamation marks, her face a mask of stone. She bent over the cooler, rummaged through the ice and came up with a soda.

"Aren't you going to have a beer with us?" Dagic said.

"Don't tempt her," Janey said. "She's underage."

Lara scowled. "It's not like I'm going to drive anywhere, Mom."

"Yeah, come on, Mom. She can handle it," Archie said.

"Alright, just one."

Dagic held up his Dale's Pale Ale. "Do you like pale ales? This one's decent,"

"That's O.K. I don't really want one," she said.

Ducharme called everyone to dinner, dished out platefuls of Two-Step along with a piece of pita bread. People settled against the canoe, blew on their steaming plates.

He dished his own and sat on the ground next to Dagic. The Croat was spreading margarine on his bread with a long double-edged knife.

"That's an impressive looking knife," he said. "Looks like a Fairbairn-Sykes fighting knife."

Dagic raised an eyebrow. "You know your knives."

"Used by the British commandos in World War II. Where'd you get it?"

"Ebay."

"Mind if I see it?"

Dagic passed him the knife. Immediately, Ducharme felt the weight of it, easily twice as heavy as his plastic river knife. He ran his finger across the sharpened edges. The leather handle smelled of sweat.

"This is a good knife to have on the river," he said. "If you capsize and your feet get tangled in rope, you don't have to look to see which is the sharpened edge."

Dagic nodded. "How'd you lose your finger?"

"A stupid accident."

He handed Dagic back his knife.

"Better be careful," the Croat said with a smile. He wiped it off on his pants leg, put it back in its sheath.

Dinner consumed and the dishes cleaned, everyone leaned back against the canoes. The craggy face of the Sierrita de Guadelupe glowed bright orange, reflecting the sun now gone behind the mountains on the American side. The shadow line, like a reverse curtain, rose from the bottom until the face was a solid, black mass against the blueing sky.

"Could you imagine if they'd run the wall through here?" Peter said.

"It would have ruined everything." Archie said.

"Consider yourselves lucky we're even allowed to camp on the Mexican side," Ducharme said. "It may not always be this way."

One by one, people returned to their tents. He stowed away the food to make sure the resident jumping mice didn't get into it. Then, he retired to his canoe where it sat upright by the shore. He unrolled his sleeping bag beneath the center thwart, rolled up his shirt to serve as a pillow and slipped inside. He lay on his back looking at the stars, weighing the events of the day. There had been no major squabbles. No one flipped their canoe. All in all, things were going pretty well. In the distance, the Rio Grande chattered over the rocks, as happy a sound as he'd ever known.

|Eleven|

Gallagher sat in the open door to his Airstream nursing a sore jaw and wounded pride. He'd get that river guide back. It was only a matter of time. But right now, he had to find a new place to park his trailer. He couldn't afford another night at the Big Bend RV Resort.

He ambled over to the restaurant for a cup of coffee, picked up a copy of the *Big Bend News* and sat at one of the Formica tables. The front page article was on a group called the West Texas Border Brigade, a volunteer group whose mission was to stop illegal immigration through "education and assisting law enforcement." They boasted of volunteers coming from all over the country, of more than one hundred illegals reported to authorities in just the past two months.

In that moment, he saw his purpose in life. His days as a ranch hand were done. He had no family of his own. But he could help stop the invasion that was taking place on the border. And he wouldn't have to go far to do it.

Using the office computer, he accessed the Brigade website and filled out the online form. Employment—none. Address—unknown. Of all the jobs in the world, this was one where those facts shouldn't matter.

The next afternoon, he got a call from brigade

headquarters in El Paso inviting him to come in for an interview. He promised to be there the next day.

"Headquarters" turned out to be a restaurant near the airport. Gallagher spotted two heavyset men with white whiskers—Hoffman and Neubauer—and introduced himself.

"Danny Gallagher. I sure am glad to be here," he said.

"Glad to have you," Hoffman said. "Order yourself a cup of coffee."

After exchanging a few pleasantries, Hoffman studied Gallagher's application. "No address for you?"

"I've got me an Airstreamer. My address is wherever I park it. Lately, I've been staying at the State Park over in Big Bend, but I can't stay there much longer. I'd need someplace to park wherever I'm stationed. Prefer that to be free."

Hoffman nodded. "'Employed—No. Last employment —ranch hand, Leaton Ranch, Fort Davis.' Do you have a reference up there?"

"I'd have to look that up."

"Never mind."

Hoffman scanned further down. "U.S. Army, four years. Were you stationed overseas?"

"Yes, sir. Second Cav, Vilsack, Germany."

"Honorably discharged?"

"Not exactly."

"A long time ago, right?"

Hoffman explained what the Border Brigade did, emphasizing that they did not make physical contact with illegals. "We're an extra set of eyes and ears for the Border Patrol. That's as far as it goes. We see a suspect, we call it in."

"I understand."

"You will be allowed to carry a sidearm, but no rifles. That sidearm is purely for your own protection."

Hoffman went on to say that they'd been having a lot of trouble with illegals crossing the river around Presidio and trespassing on private ranches. "They're making a helluva mess. We've made arrangements with a number of ranchers to patrol their property. We need another man down there. Is that something that would interest you?"

"Oh, yes, sir. I know that territory well."

"There's one rancher would probably let you park that trailer on his property. I don't know as he has an electrical hookup."

"Oh, I can get by," he said.

"I trust you've had experience operating an ATV?"

"All day, every day."

"Good. You'll be partnering with another volunteer on your patrols. Goes by the code name of 'Blood Hound.' Do you have one you'd like to use?"

He thought for a moment. "How about 'El Chompo'?"

Hoffman and Neubauer exchanged glances.

"Well, El Champo," Hoffman said, "welcome aboard."

***

Monday morning, Gallagher waxed his moustache, strapped on his pistol, and stopped by the Big 5 in El Paso to purchase a full set of camo gear. Airstream in tow, he drove the highway back east through the desert, musing aloud in his high-pitched voice about the would-be border jumpers just across the river. "Yes, siree, there's gonna be a new set of eyes on you now. You're gonna wish you'd stayed home with mama*cita*."

Four hours later, he pulled into the brigade depot in Redford. There, under a shed roof, stood four camo-painted ATVs.

"Hoo hoo, look at this," he said. "We got ourselves a tank platoon."

A man stepped out of the shade and offered a meaty hand, his smile barely nudging the edges of his salt-and-pepper moustache.

"Bruce Miller. They call me the Blood Hound."

"Danny Gallagher. El Chompo."

The Hound pointed to the stable of ATVs. "This is what we take out on patrol. They're all Kawasaki 800s. Are you familiar with that machine?"

"Know it by heart. I rode a Cow my last job."

"They're equipped with CB radios. We call into headquarters every time we head out and every time we get back. If we see someone suspicious, we radio it in and they call the Border Patrol. We do not engage with illegals, did they make that clear?"

"They did."

The Hound checked his watch. "We're scheduled to meet Mr. Weaver at his ranch in half-an-hour. It's back up the road about two miles. Do you mind riding shotgun?"

As they motored along the River Road, the Hound questioned him about his past. "You say you worked a ranch up at Fort Davis?"

"Yes, sir. The Leaton Ranch just north of town."

"I've seen the head gate. They treat you good up there?"

"Mrs. Leaton runs the place. She treated me fine until some wetback walked in the door and offered to work for

$10 an hour."

The Hound shook his head.

"I tried to reason with her. I said this man'll be gone as soon as someone offers him $10.50. She wouldn't hear it."

"There's two theories to arguing with a woman and neither one of them works."

"Amen to that."

Randy Weaver, owner of the Double Y Ranch, stood beside his white pick-up truck. He looked about 6'2" in his stockman boots, with a straw hat curled up at the edges and the eyes of a rattlesnake. He studied a sheet of paper on which he'd written a note from his phone conversation with Hoffman.

"Blood Hound and El Chompo. Now, there's a combo you don't hear every day."

"He sniffs 'em out and I chomp 'em," Gallagher said.

Weaver smiled. "You understand there's to be no physical contact with illegals. I don't need any trouble with the courts."

"Roger that," the Hound said.

Weaver motioned to his truck. "Unless y'all want to get real cozy, I suggest you follow me in your ATV. I've got more than a mile of riverfront property. We'll take a tour of that, then circle back along the highway."

It was getting on toward evening, the light going ever earlier as October gave way to November. They crested a rise and the river came into view, heading straight south then turning a hairpin and running back north. Weaver stopped at the bend and walked out to the bluff.

"That's our savior right there," Weaver said. "The only thing that keeps us from being overrun. I believe God put that river there to separate the white races from the darker ones."

Gallagher nodded. It made sense if you thought about it.

"As you can see, it's thick with creosote on the other side," Weaver went on. "There's a million places to hide and just as many to cross. It'd be one thing if they just passed over my land, but they keep pulling down my fence. A Hereford finds a break and she's halfway to Presidio before I find out."

Gallagher studied the terrain. "Best chance to see 'em is when they cross the river?"

"Yes, sir, but they mostly cross at night. Did they give y'all night vision goggles?"

"They're talking about buying some," the Hound said. "We ain't got 'em yet."

A mile further along they came to a dry wash that entered the river from out of the mountains. Weaver pointed out his window.

"Footprints," the Hound said. "See 'em in the sand?"

"I see 'em."

Weaver circled back toward the ranch, paralleling the barbed wire fence line that bordered the road. At the bottom of a swale, he parked the truck and got out. Two strands of wire hung limp from a post.

"This is just what I'm talking about," he said. "One of my cows gets in the road and she's likely to get hit. Worse, somebody runs into her and gets killed and I'm sued for negligence."

"We can sure put a stop to that," Gallagher said.

They arrived back at the ranch house just before dark. Weaver asked if they had any questions.

"Did Mr. Hoffman mention about my needing some

place to park my trailer?" Gallagher said.

Weaver frowned. "He mentioned something about that. I don't have a hook up except at the house."

"That's alright. I got me a generator."

"How long are you planning to stay?"

"Just until the tourists leave in December. Then I can get a campsite over at the state park. They're not too picky about that two-week limit once the tourists leave."

Weaver sighed. "Alright. You can pull it up there near the barn."

"Thank you, sir."

As the two volunteers rode back to Redford, Gallagher broke into song. "*Coyotes howl and the cattle prowl out on the Great Divide, never done no wrong singing a song, as down the trail I ride...*"

The Hound looked over. "Are you singing because of our mission or because of the free rent?"

"Pardner, I'd have to say it's a little of both."

|Twelve|

Janey awoke in the light of early dawn, Lara asleep beside her, her phone beneath her limp hand. Janey lifted it up to check the time. 6 am. Robbie had said he was going to wake everyone by then, but save for the snoring of someone in a nearby tent, the campground was silent. She pulled on her clothes, unzipped the tent, and walked over to the kitchen area. Robbie was nowhere to be seen. Somewhere across the river, a bird was singing in a wonderful downward spiraling trill. She slung her camera over her shoulder and walked to the shore. There was Robbie, asleep in his canoe pulled up on the rocks.

"Robbie."

He didn't stir. She poked his naked shoulder.

"Robbie."

He opened his eyes. "What time is it?"

"It's after 6."

"Shit." He sat up and stared around him. "I was having a bad dream."

"Oh, no. What was it?"

"I need to get up. Thanks for waking me."

He reached into his pack and got out a plastic pillbox. He opened the box, picked out two pills and reached for his water. He glanced at Janey. She turned away, secretly

100

glad she was not the only one who needed to start her day with pharmaceuticals.

"What is that beautiful bird song across the river?" she said.

He listened. "That's a canyon wren."

"It's really lovely."

"River guides brag about their imitations of that song. I haven't learned it yet."

"Oh, that's right. You're new out here."

As Robbie leaned forward to put on his shirt, she noticed the pale skin on the back of his neck.

"Did you used to have long hair?" she said.

"Yes, why do you ask?"

"Nothing. I just noticed it."

He pulled himself out of his sleeping bag and stood in his boxer shorts. His sleepy-eyed, buff physique reminded her of Jake Gyllenhall in his war movie days.

"I'm going to take a walk along the river," she said.

"Breakfast will be ready in half-an-hour, " he said. "Be back by then. And watch out for snakes."

She headed along the bank, eyes on the ground. She hadn't gone twenty yards when she practically ran into Janko crouched in his undershorts.

"God, you scared me!" she said. "I didn't know you were there."

"No problem," he said. "Are you out for a walk?"

"Yes, I'm birdwatching."

He stood, revealing his hairy chest and muscled torso. "Mind if I join you? I'll just put on some clothes."

Politeness dictated that she accept the offer. But she was a little unnerved by this man. She could tell by the glances he'd thrown her way that he was attracted to her.

But she was not in a mood just now to deal with that. She wanted just to walk free, to look for birds.

She held up her camera. "I'd prefer to go alone," she said. "Easier to sneak up on them."

"Suit yourself."

Approaching a low hill, she heard a nasal peep from beneath a mesquite tree. Another bird responded a short distance away—obviously a mating pair of something. She maneuvered around the tree and glimpsed a quail with a grey back and a maroon-banded head. It was clearly a male, its forehead topped by a beautiful black tassel. It scurried out from under the tree into the underbrush. She followed with her camera, hoping for a clear shot. Halfway up the hill, the quail and its mate took flight, gliding on stubby wings over the crest.

She strode to the top of the hill and looked back toward where she'd come. There was the camp spread out along the river, maroon tent tops visible between the shrubs. Suddenly, a man stood up in the brush, naked from the waist down. He had his back to her, but she could tell from his lumpy physique that it was Pooh Bear. He was finishing up his business, but he kept looking over his shoulder and scratching one of his buttocks. Finally, he pulled up his pants and walked back to his tent.

She continued on along the crest of the hill, coming back to camp from upriver. Everyone was awake now, standing around the kitchen drinking coffee.

"Did you see anything interesting?" Robbie asked.

"You might say so." She thought to mention her sighting of Pooh Bear, but kept quiet about it. "I saw a beautiful grey quail with a tassel on its head."

"That's a Gambel's quail," he said.

"So handsome."

Lara came out of the tent with a sour look on her face. "God, who was that snoring last night?"

Her question was met with silence, until Parker guiltily raised her hand. "I'm afraid that was me. My husband says I could wake the dead."

Janey felt bad for Parker, but admired her for fessing up.

Pooh Bear came out of the bush and whispered something to Archie, who burst out laughing.

"Pooh Bear sat on a cactus!" Archie said.

Peter blushed. "Oh, tell the world about it."

"You sat on a cactus?" Robbie said. "How did that happen?"

"He was taking a shit," Archie said.

"You're supposed to be using the Honey Pot," Robbie said.

"Believe me, I'll do that next time."

Janey warmed to see Lara laughing with the others. Her daughter rarely found anything adults did or said to be funny.

Delicious smells arose from the kitchen. Robbie cooked bacon over one burner, pancakes on another. He added four blueberries to each pancake, then served them hot off the griddle. The maple syrup might be fake, but Janey couldn't remember anything tasting so good.

It didn't take long before she felt the urge to use the Honey Pot. She had been avoiding this as long as possible, but time was up. She waited until she saw someone lower the paddle and come back up the trail. She gritted her teeth and ventured out.

The bucket looked so small, she thought it might

topple over if she sat on it. Were the others lighter than she was? No. She dropped her drawers, raised the lid and hurriedly sat down. She'd never been embarrassed about defecating, but now she felt she was adding too much volume to what was already there. Would people notice? After she was done, she scooped in an extra cup of sawdust to cover things up. She washed her hands and walked away. Thank God that was over with.

She and Lara packed their clothes into their waterproof duffels and took down the tent without argument. They carried the gear to the canoes and began tying and strapping it to the thwarts. By the time the sun hit the river, everyone was ready to go.

"Folks, we're going to be paddling 17 miles today," Robbie said. "There's only one named rapid, Maravilas Creek. There's a large rock in the middle of the river that's often hidden by a pillow of water. If you hit that rock, you will likely capsize and maybe pin your canoe. So follow me when we go into the rapid and stay to the left."

She felt a stirring in her bowels at the mention of the danger. Would she and Lara crash and be humiliated in front of everyone? People would be angry that they slowed the group down. She imagined the men would all get through, though Archie and Pooh Bear appeared not to be strong paddlers. Maybe they would crash, too.

The group headed downriver to the farewell song of a canyon wren. The sky was a lovely shade of pale blue, the air pleasantly cool. A solitary mountain rose to the Mexican side of the river, its peak aglow in the morning sun.

Five miles along, the layered ledges of Maravilas Creek came into view.

"Here's our rapid," Robbie called. "Remember about that boulder."

The rush of falling water grew louder. She stayed close behind Janko and Richard, the canoes picking up speed as the muddy river sprouted tongues of white. There was the boulder in midstream, just as Robbie said. She called to Lara. "Go to the left."

For the first time, Lara paddled with conviction. Janey followed by paddling hard on the opposite side, and the heavy canoe miraculously responded. They whizzed past the boulder and bounced over a series of waves. Just like that, they were through.

"We did it!" Janey cried.

"Don't get your hopes up," Lara answered.

They paddled on into open country, an area known as Las Vegas de Los Ladrones, Outlaw Flats. There was not a building in sight, and no sound, save for Archie's distant chatter. Now and then, Janko would turn around and look Archie's way. The talk was clearly bothering him.

They stopped for lunch on a gravel bar with a magnificent view of a distant butte. There were so many different rock formations along this river, all begging to be photographed. She worried she would run her camera battery down before they were halfway through.

Robbie laid out a lunch of packaged turkey, cheese, and lettuce and tomato. The turkey and tomato were equally tasteless, but Janey was so famished, she inhaled her sandwich, downed a box of grape juice, and ate six mini-chocolate chip cookies.

After lunch, Robbie invited everyone to take a half-hour nap. Instead, Janey ventured into the flats in search of more birds. Precious few emerged in the heat of the day, but just as she was about to give up, a road runner darted into view. She waited for the bird to pause in its hunting, held her breath, and snapped one picture. On replay, it proved to be perfect.

Afternoon brought more flat water. Her strength began to wane in the heat and she found herself wishing she could trade places with Parker in the bow of Robbie's canoe. Archie and Richard passed her, but she was not going to call for a break unless and until one of the men did. Somehow, she was able to find a second wind, and when the campsite finally appeared, and she beached the canoe, pride reigned over exhaustion. She and Lara emptied their canoe before anyone else's and carried it up to the campsite to serve as one of the couches.

"That was quick," Robbie said. "Thank you."

The fact that he'd noticed her effort and thanked her for it brought unexpected warmth to her soul. Despite everything, they were creating a bond. Or was she imagining things?

|Thirteen|

While the others put up their tents, Dagic unrolled his sleeping bag on the ground. He retrieved a plastic bottle from his duffel bag and brought it to the kitchen where Ducharme was preparing dinner.

"Vodka for you, Robbie?"

"Sure. There are juice boxes in that container. Why don't you get me an apple juice and put a little of that in a cup."

Dagic mixed up the drink and handed it to him. "Ziveli!" he said, giving the Croation version of "cheers."

Ducharme took a sip. "Mmm, that tastes like a good vodka."

Dagic smiled. "Stoli."

Ducharme finished his drink and set the cup beside the stove. "How long ago did you move to the States?"

"About ten years."

"Why Chicago?"

"Friends."

He stirred the stew. "Why did you leave Croatia?"

"No work after the war."

"The Serbo-Croation War?"

"What else?"

Ducharme nodded. "What is it you do for work?"

"Carpentry."

"I'd think there'd be work for a carpenter in a country rebuilding after a war."

Dagic poured himself another drink. "And why is it you left Georgia?"

"I wanted to start my own company. There wasn't any more room for a commercial outfitter on the river we ran, so I decided to look elsewhere."

"You have contacts here?"

"No. I've pretty much started from scratch."

The water came to a boil. He poured in yellow rice. "Did you fight in the war, Janko?"

"No."

"I wondered, because you would have been in your early twenties then, right?"

"I didn't join."

"I've read some about that conflict. It sounded like the Serbs committed some horrible atrocities against the Croats. The Vukovar massacre."

Dagic shrugged. "Everyone's had their massacres. You massacred your Indians. The Indians massacred other Indians..."

Ducharme was surprised that Dagic dismissed the widespread killing of his innocent countrymen. But he had a point about the universality of bad behavior in war. Best to change the subject.

"So where is this Black River?" he said.

"Pardon?"

"You put on your application that you'd canoed a Class III river called the Black."

"It's north of Chicago."

"Up in Michigan?"

"Yes."

"There are lots of Black Rivers, but I haven't heard of any Class III rivers in the upper Midwest."

People sometimes confused the rating of a whitewater river or exaggerated its difficulty. But something in Dagic' eyes convinced Ducharme that the man was making this river up.

Janey walked up looking refreshed. Dagic offered her a drink, which she politely refused. One by one, the others appeared. Archie struck up a conversation with Janey. He asked straight off if she was married, not in a tone that suggested an interest in her availability, but strictly as a matter of information.

"I'm separated," she said.

"How long were you married?"

"Eighteen years."

"Are you working?"

"Yes, I'm a career counselor at Georgia Tech."

Archie mulled that over. "Would you advise others to do what you did?"

"Career wise?"

"Yes."

"It's got its pluses and minuses."

Peter entered the conversation. "I went to Georgia Tech. A long time ago."

"What was your degree?" Janey asked.

"Electrical engineering."

"And now you're a realtor!"

He nodded bashfully.

"Pooh Bear realized he wasn't built to crawl through tight spaces," Archie said.

"No, I found out I didn't like working for other people."

Parker jumped in. "You found the money is better in real estate. At least it has been in Cary."

The realtors launched into a conversation about the ups and downs of the real estate market. Ducharme noticed Janey looking off to where Dagic was talking with Lara. He had a charming smile that held Lara in rapt attention. It was quite an image—the tall, dark stranger and the innocent young blonde. Janey looked uneasy.

He sent out the call for dinner.

"This is what I call Mother-in-Law Stew," he said, as he ladled his entree onto plates.

"You're married?" Parker said.

"No, but I learned it from someone who is."

After everyone was served, he sat on the ground and leaned back against the canoe. A thin bank of clouds, upturned at the front like a tablecloth suspended in mid-toss, hung above the cliffs of the Sierrita de Guadalupes. As the sun set, the group marveled about how the clouds turned from orange to purple to grey.

"Enjoy the view while you can," he said. "Tomorrow, we'll be entering the big canyons. You won't see a far horizon for another three days."

"That sounds like a warning," Archie said.

"No, I think you'll get to like it."

He gathered up the dishes and carried them down to the river. As a guide, he didn't ask others to help him with the clean-up, but he was always pleased if someone did. That someone was Dagic.

They squatted side by side, he washing and Dagic rinsing. "Are you happy with Richard as a paddler?" he said.

Dagic nodded. "He's O.K."

"I'll be switching off paddlers now and again to try out different combinations."

"Don't give me Peter or Archie."

"Listen, we've all got to work together. You look to be one of the strongest paddlers, so I may put you with one of the less able people. That might be Peter or Archie, or it might be someone else."

Dagic frowned. "I'll take Peter, then, but that Archie never stops talking."

"Does it bother you?" he said.

"You don't hear him?"

"I hear him."

Dagic motioned to the sky. "We're in this beautiful place. We should be quiet."

He couldn't argue that. "If he keeps it up, I'll speak to him about it."

***

At breakfast, Ducharme explained what they would encounter in the morning's paddle. They would continue on through Outlaw Flats with only one rapid of consequence. But there would be several of what he called "cane shots" that could be very tricky.

"River cane is like bamboo," he explained. "It grows in thick strands along the banks, and on sharp bends where the bank is eroded, it can lean out 10-15 feet over the river. If you run into that cane, it can easily capsize you. You need to stay to the *inside* of those bends, away from the cane. Do you understand?"

The group responded with sober nods.

They launched with the morning sun behind them, a

curious prospect for a river that ultimately drained east into the Gulf of Mexico. But that was the quixotic nature of the Big Bend, running north one minute and south the next. On this morning, the river lay mirror smooth with a bright green border of river cane on both shores. Above the cane, the land sloped up to a band of cream-colored cliffs that ran in a line along the horizon.

Rounding a bend, they came upon a copper-headed Merganser leading six ducklings upstream. Most ducks would have hidden in the cane, but the Mergansers broke into a frantic upstream scoot, their legs churning the water like high-speed paddle wheelers.

Parker laughed. "I guess they haven't evolved far enough to understand that canoeists are harmless."

A mile beyond, they came to their first cane shot. Ducharme waved his paddle in the air to alert the group. The channel was narrow, barely a dozen yards wide, with the current running toward the outside of the bend and its overhanging wall of cane. He called on Parker to "draw left", which involved planting one's paddle far out to one side and drawing it toward the canoe. That turned the bow toward the inside of the bend, and to get the stern to follow, Ducharme executed a "sweep," a wide stroke on the opposite side. With a few hard strokes, they drove past the cane with yards to spare.

Dagic followed the same route. Richard pulled well in the bow, but Dagic failed to execute a sweep. The stern of the canoe swung into the cane. After some loud swearing, he came out the other side, covered in cane seeds, but otherwise none the worse for wear. Then came Janey and Lara. Ducharme could see from the start that they were too far to the outside of the bend. Janey called on Lara to draw, but it was too late. They crashed into the cane and tipped over.

Lara bobbed to the surface just downstream of Janey. "Jesus Christ, Mom!" she sputtered.

"Hold onto your paddles!" Ducharme shouted.

He and Parker maneuvered their canoe to intercept Janey's. They pointed the bow of their canoe to strike the overturned boat amidships and drove it to shore. Lara and Janey climbed out on the bank, wet and shaken.

"Everybody alright?" Ducharme said.

Lara scowled. "I lost my hat."

Janey drained the water out of her pants. "You needed to draw harder, honey."

"I did! You went too far to the outside."

Ducharme stepped in. "You both could have run that better. Janey, you need to set up to the inside of those turns before you enter them. And, Lara, you've got to draw harder in the bow."

Dagic and Richard pulled up, the former holding Lara's hat. "I believe this is yours," he said.

Lara smiled. "Oh, my God, thank you."

The two other canoes arrived.

"Is everyone OK?" Archie asked.

"We're fine," Janey said.

Ducharme called the group together. "Now you know the strength of the current," he said. "You've got to look ahead and imagine where the current is going to want to push you. You can't wait until you're pushed over to the side."

Janey and Lara righted the canoe, drained out the water, and took their seats. The trip resumed.

A mile later, the rock outcropping marking the

entrance to Big Canyon Rapid rose to the left. Ducharme slowed his canoe and waited for the others to catch up.

"We've got fast water ahead," he said. "There's some big boulders on the right hand side of the channel, so you're going to have to paddle hard to the inside, just like last time."

The river picked up speed, the roar of falling water rising in the air. Dead ahead, water pillowed up behind a barely submerged line of boulders. He barked out a command.

"Draw left!"

Parker reacted and they scooted passed the boulders and plowed through the waves below.

"Eddy out!"

An eddy was a pocket of still water behind a rock or to the inside of a sharp bend. Eddies could be as small as a bathtub or as big as a garage. To "eddy out" was to turn the canoe into the still water with the bow aimed upstream. It was a good technique to recover if your boat was full of water or to watch the others come through a rapid.

One by one, the boats came into view—Dagic and Richard, Janey and Lara. Lara leaned out and executed a strong draw in the bow, pulling the canoe well clear of the rocks. Sitting bolt upright in the last canoe, Peter executed a weak draw. The canoe bounced off the boulder and very nearly flipped. He pulled into the eddy looking ashen-faced.

"Peter, you've got to commit yourself to the draw," Ducharme said. "Do you understand what that means?"

Peter turned sideways, dipped his paddle in the water and moved it toward the hull.

"Yes, but *commit* to it. Lean out, get your arms high and pull that paddle towards you *hard*."

He tried again, moving the bow a little further.

"Better," Ducharme said. "Remember to pull the paddle straight toward the boat."

They set back on the river, slipping into a towering canyon. Ducharme stopped paddling and waited for the canoeists to come together. "Folks, the top of this canyon is 1,500 feet above us," he said. "That's taller than the Empire State Building."

They stared up in silence. Everyone except Archie.

"Pooh Bear, if you jumped from the top, it would impress us all," he said. "You could make up for hitting that rock."

Dagic glared at Archie. "Don't you ever shut up?"

No one spoke a word. Janey looked particularly shocked. Ducharme decided to break the ice. "Let's take a lunch break," he said.

Conversation was subdued as he set out the lunch fixings. People sat in pairs. Dagic went down to the shore and ate by himself. Ducharme joined him.

"I've got an idea for the group I think you'll like," he said. "Until then, try and be polite. We've got three more days on the river."

Dagic nodded. "More fun?"

"Always."

***

After lunch, Ducharme outlined his plan for the afternoon. "We're going to try something called a silent paddle. I learned this years ago on a rafting trip down the Grand

Canyon. I hesitate to use the word 'spiritual', but that's what it can be like. The rule is that no one talks until we reach our campsite. There are no rapids on this next stretch of the river, so you don't need to be giving commands. Try to absorb everything around you. Are you all game for this?"

Heads nodded all around.

"About two miles down, there's a cave on the left called La Cueva de la Puerta Grande," he said. "I read that there's evidence this cave was used by Native Americans as far back as 10,000 years B.C. You'll notice the ceiling is charred from old fires. Try to imagine all the people using this through the ages, how they must have survived in this harsh environment."

They set back on the river. The change was immediate. Everyone's faces seemed to be directed outwards. The only sound was the dripping of water from the paddles. High overhead, vultures circled on thermal currents rising off of the cliffs. At one point, a falcon flew out from its perch on the canyon wall, circled once in the thin band of blue, then merged again with the rock.

At a bend in the river, along a rock formation, he spotted the top of the cave behind the mesquite trees. He directed the group toward shore. They beached the canoes and followed him through the dry grass. Near the entrance to the cave, he stopped and raised his hand. A rattlesnake was sunning at the base of the rock wall, not ten yards away. It was a western diamondback with beautiful amber markings. The snake either didn't see them or wasn't bothered by their presence. Ducharme waited for the group to get a good look, then walked on past. The snake never moved.

Inside the cave, the air was cool and dry, the light fading to total darkness at the back. Ducharme pointed at the charred ceiling. Richard knelt down and picked through the scattered rocks on the floor. They stood in silence, a sense of wonder hopefully sinking in, when someone farted. It was a high, tight fart that the guilty party tried to suppress. Lara held her hand over her mouth and started to giggle. Then Archie, then Peter. Soon everyone cracked up.

"Alright," Ducharme said, "The silent paddle is over, so to speak. Who cut the cheese, anyway?"

The group set back on the river in high spirits. Ducharme felt happy that he had defused an ugly situation, the first of the trip and, hopefully, the last. They reached the campsite, everyone lending a hand to set up the kitchen and the couch. They then went off to pitch their tents. The clicking of tent poles mingled with light disagreements.

"I think this pole goes in this sleeve."

"No, it doesn't. It's this one."

Ducharme loved this peaceful stage of his trips. People usually spent some time unpacking their gear and changing clothes, maybe reading a book or taking a quick nap. In an hour or so, when the smells of dinner wafted through the campsite, they would come into the kitchen area. Someone would start a conversation, usually about work or family. For Ducharme, a man who had never worked professionally other than as a river guide and had no family of his own, it was a time to listen. Would he ever have a job like theirs? Did he even want one? Would he ever have a family?

Richard brought out his guitar and started playing a

tune. It sounded like a polka until he sang the lyrics in Spanish.

"What's that you're singing?" Ducharme asked.

"It's called 'La Jaula de Oro,' 'The Golden Cage.' It's about an illegal immigrant who starts a new life in the U.S. only to find himself trapped, unable to go home."

"I can relate to that."

"How so?"

"It's a long story."

Richard nodded, put his guitar back in its case.

|Fourteen|

In the early morning hours, Sayda and Kelin stepped off the bus in the Ciudad Tecan Uman, Guatemala. They had ridden two buses from Honduras, sleeping all the way from Guatemala City. She looked down the street to the north, saw the gap in the treeline. That, she prayed, would be the Suchiate River, the border between Guatemala and Mexico. She motioned to Kelin to follow.

"Wait a minute," he said. "You don't know where you're going."

She pointed. "This is north, idiot."

In truth, she was terrified. Neither she nor Kelin had ever left Honduras. She had never broken a law, never lied to an authority figure. She would have to do both if they ever hoped to make it to the United States.

In their small backpacks, Sayda and Kelin carried everything their mother had deemed essential for a month-long journey. For Sayda, that was:

- a poncho
- a jacket
- two pairs of underpants
- a bra
- one pair of blue jeans

- a long-sleeved shirt
- a T-shirt
- a dozen tampons
- a toothbrush and comb
- a cell phone

In the zippered pocket of the top flap, folded inside a plastic baggie, she kept the most important item of all—the newspaper article describing the killing of her father. This was to be presented to any authorities who questioned the purpose of their journey, most importantly, to the Americans who would ultimately decide whether they could stay in that country.

As she stepped between the buildings at the end of the street, she saw the river before them. The surface was peppered with rafts made of giant truck inner tubes, piloted by men using long poles made from mangrove trees. As they reached the river's edge, a man called out to her.

"Over here. I will take you. Only 24 pesos each."

Kelin started in his direction, but Sayda held him back. She'd seen her mother bargain down fruit sellers in the market many times.

"That's too much," she said. "We'll find someone for less."

"Alright, 18 pesos. Get on."

Sayda and Kelin stepped onto the wooden boards lashed to the inner tubes.

"Move to the front," the man said.

When he'd loaded on two boys with bicycles, the riverman pushed the raft into the Suchiate. Sayda felt the tires dip into the current, heard the muffled crunch of the pole against the gravely bottom. From the trees along the river came the two-note hoot of the motmot and the steady rasp of the toucan. For the first time since they'd left San Pedro Sul, she allowed herself to believe she would live to see another sunrise.

She looked behind her to the east. The massive silhouette of the Santa Maria volcano loomed against the sky. She shuddered at the sight of it, a dormant volcano that could come to life at any time. Below it hung a thin layer of clouds—heaven, she'd been told by the nuns at her school. But from here, she could see it was nothing more than a cloud, here one minute, gone the next.

"Where are you two going?" the riverman said.

"North," Sayda answered.

"El gabacho?"

She was silent. Her mother told her not to divulge information about their destination to anyone they didn't have to, lest they suspect they were carrying a large sum of money. But Kelin couldn't keep quiet.

"We're going to Texas," he said. "We have an uncle there."

The riverman nodded to the rafts coming the other way. "Do you see all these rafts coming back?" he said. "Half the people on them are returning to their homes after trying to get to the States. If the American government doesn't send you back, the Mexican government will. You will be very lucky to get across and stay across."

"We have a guide to help us," Kelin said.

The riverman smiled. "There are lots of people who will be happy to take your money. All of it. If you make it to the Rio Bravo, you won't find anyone like me. The new breed of coyotes has no soul. The Yankees neither. Times have changed."

They reached the far shore and stepped onto Mexican soil. Boys with bicycle taxis called to her. "This way! This way!"

She told them she needed to find the bus to Oaxaca.

"You must go to Tapachula for that," the nearest one said. "I will take you. Fifteen pesos each."

The bus station in the center of town was crowded with men and women carrying suitcases. Sayda felt exposed with only her backpack and no adult by her side. She asked Kelin for the bills he kept hidden in his shoe, approached the ticket counter and asked for two tickets to Oaxaca, second class.

"Twelve hundred pesos," the agent said.

She had never held that amount of money in her hand, had to study the notes to make sure what they were. The agent looked annoyed.

"That one," Kelin said, pointing to the 200 pesos notes with the picture of the nun. "Give him six."

They bought their tickets and wandered through the station. A convenience store sold candy, crackers and soft drinks. Kelin walked in. "I'm going to buy a Coke," he said.

Sayda grabbed him by the arm. "No, we have water," she said. "Don't waste your money on things you don't need."

Kelin pulled away. "Don't tell me what to do."

He approached the cooler, studied the prices. He came back to Sayda empty-handed. "Those are way too expensive," he said.

When they boarded the bus, Sayda led Kelin to the back where they wouldn't be noticed. The bus was much fancier than anything they'd ridden in San Pedro Sula. As well as being comfortable, the high-backed seats hid them from view. You could barely hear the motor start.

All morning, they rode through the green fields of Chiapas, the endless Sierra Madre Mountain range rising in the distance. It was all going so well, then outside the town of Chahuites, the bus stopped. Sayda's grandfather had warned them there might be immigration checkpoints.

"If they try to send you back, show them the article about your father," he said. "If that doesn't work, offer to pay them."

The officer came down the aisle, dark, heavy-set, terrifying.

"Identification, please."

Sayda and Kelin produced their student IDs.

"Hondurans," he said. "Fifteen years old. Where are you going?"

At once, Sayda answered "Oaxaca" and Kelin said, "The U.S."

"Do you have green cards? Visas for the U.S.?"

They shook their heads.

"Come with me."

Sayda flushed with shame as they were led off the bus. The door closed behind them and the bus pulled away. The policeman led them to a small booth. He wrote down the information from their IDs and handed them back.

"You are here illegally," he said. "You must go back to Honduras."

"But, sir, we have tickets for Oaxaca," Sayda said.

"Doesn't matter. You don't have permission to be in Mexico and certainly not the U.S."

"Sir, please, I have something to show you."

She dug the plastic bag out of her backpack, unfolded the newspaper article, and handed it to the officer.

"Our father was murdered by the gangs," she said. "We are seeking asylum in the States. We can't go back."

The officer read the article. "I'm sorry about this, but you will not get asylum in the U.S. They only grant it for political reasons. This is crime, not politics."

Kelin glanced at Sayda.

"Pay him," he mouthed.

Sayda sushed him. She reached under her shirt, felt the seam in her bra. She pulled out six tightly folded 500 peso notes and handed them to the officer.

"Please," she said. "We can't go back."

The officer took the bills, unfolded them, then stuck them in his shirt pocket.

"Go into town," he said. "There is another bus to Oaxaca tomorrow."

|Fifteen|

Gallagher was well pleased with his new home site on the Weaver ranch. From his Airstream, he could see down to the Rio Grande and across to the brushy hills in Mexico. To announce his presence to would-be border crossers, he tied his American flag to a length of rusted steel pipe and anchored it in a pile of rocks. From scraps of wood found around Weaver's barn, he fashioned a stand on which he set his binoculars, pistol, and walkie talkie. Every morning, he saluted the flag, then poured himself a cup of coffee and settled into a lawn chair behind the stand.

"Yes, sir," he announced as he peered through his binocs. "Ain't no one gonna overrun this outpost. Remember the Alamo!"

He started off his day by radioing in to the Blood Hound. "Ah, Blood Hound, this is El Chompo checking in. Do you read me?"

Blood Hound eventually informed him that it was not necessary to call in every morning and that the Hound liked to sleep a bit later than El Chompo.

Then came the hours of scanning the far bank. Most days, he saw no one except the young boy who brought his goats down to drink out of the river. The boy was initially startled to see the shirtless man in the cowboy hat staring at him through binoculars. Upon being spotted, Gallagher pointed with two fingers at his own eyes, then pointed to the boy.

"I got eyes on you, amigo."

The boy ignored him.

The West Texas Border Brigade volunteers were given few specifics on how and when to search for illegals. The Hound liked to go out first thing in the morning or just before sunset. That was when the light was low and he could make out footprints most easily. The first day, the Hound showed up in the evening.

"Let's go cut some sign," he said.

While the Hound steered the ATV along the bluffs overlooking the river, Gallagher chatted on about illegals.

"They live like animals, so they can afford to work for nothing," he said.

The Hound nodded. "I hear that."

He and his first wife had lived most of their years in Detroit, before the auto industry moved to Mexico. "Work dried up, my wife left me, so I moved down here to Redford, got remarried, and decided to do something for my country."

Gallagher brightened. "Hey, did you hear the joke about the two Mexicans walking down the road?"

"Careful," the Hound said. "My wife is Mexican."

"Anyway, Pepe and Jose are walking down the road. Pepe smells something awful and says, 'Jose, did you sheet in your pants?' Jose says, 'No man, I didn't sheet in my pants.' They keep on walking. Flies start buzzing around Jose's ass. Pepe says again, 'Man, are you sure you didn't sheet in your pants?' Jose says, 'No, man, I already told you.' Finally, Pepe can't stand the smell any longer. He pulls down Pepe's pants and finds them full of dried up shit. Pepe says, 'Why did you lie to me, man, you did sheet in your pants.' Jose says, 'Oh, I thought you meant *today.*'"

The Hound managed a week smile. "Like I said, my wife is Mexican. She's a citizen, but that's where she was born."

Gallagher looked at him. "I thought you were joking."

For the first few weeks, he and the Hound surprised no one other than the occasional jack rabbit or family of javelina. Weaver discovered several more broken fence lines and convinced the men that they actually needed to go out after midnight, when the border crossers were most active. Another week of fruitless searching followed, but on the night of November 1, the Blood Hound caught a scent.

"Let's go up to that far pasture tonight. I have a feeling we may see some action."

Sure enough, they caught a group of immigrants on open ground. Gallagher got on the CB to headquarters.

"This is El Chompo. Be advised we have a group of illegals crossing the pasture at the Weaver Ranch. They appear to be headed for the River Road."

"Roger that, Chompo. Do not engage. I will call Border Patrol."

Caught in the headlights of the ATV, the immigrants decided to head back to the river.

Gallagher called out, "Get along, little doggies. No trabajo for you."

One of the men gave him the finger. That got him riled. He unholstered his pistol and fired three shots in the air. The immigrants started running.

"What the hell are you doing?" the Hound said. "Put

that damn pistol away."

"Got their attention, didn't it?"

"You do not, I repeat, do not say anything about this to the Border Patrol. We don't need to get on their bad side."

"Whatever you say, boss."

The next day, Gallagher suggested they go to the Starlight Cafe to celebrate their rout of the border crossers. They arrived in full camo gear with West Texas Border Brigade patches on their shoulders. Tourists frowned as they strode past the tables. Gallagher snapped back.

"What's the matter, hoss? You've never seen a patriot?"

He and the Hound sat at the bar. "Let's have a couple of Dos Equis. First round's on me."

A white-haired couple with acoustic guitars took the stage and began singing cowboy songs. Gallagher sang along. *"Down in the west Texas town of El Paso, I fell in love with a Mexican girl..."*

He waved his empty glass at the bartender.

"You made quick work of that," the bartender said.

"I worked up a thirst today. Chased a bunch of Jumping Beans back across the border."

"Is that right? Another one for you, sir?" the bartender said to the Hound.

He shook his head.

Three river guides arrived at the bar, including the one who'd floored Gallagher the month before. He sat next to the Blood Hound, recognized Gallagher.

"Look who's back," he said. "All decked out in a fancy uniform."

Gallagher frowned. "Hey, asshole, meet my friend, the

Blood Hound. He can sniff out chicken shit faster than a sneeze through a screen door."

The bartender got in Gallagher's face. "Am I going to have to drag you out of here again?"

He held up his hands. "No trouble here, officer."

The Hound spoke into his ear. "Seems like you've made friends all over town. Let's drink up and head out."

In the following days, Gallagher lounged in his lawn chair fighting boredom and resentment. Twice an Apache helicopter passed overhead, part of the U.S. Army's growing presence on the border. He snapped to attention and saluted. "That's what I'm talkin' about, right there!"

Once, a drone came down the river and hovered overhead as Gallagher sat in his chair nursing a bottle of tequila. He stared bleary-eyed at the machine, then saluted it, too.

A week to the day following their previous interdiction, the Blood Hound had another hunch. "Let's go out to that wash tonight," he said. "I have a feeling they'll be looking to take advantage of the full moon."

As soon as they crested the rise above the wash, they hit pay dirt. A group of illegals was trudging up the middle of the dried up stream. Gallagher at the wheel of the ATV cut them off.

"You are hereby pronounced as trespassers on the Weaver Ranch," he said.

The immigrants turned around and headed back to the river, Gallagher following close behind. Suddenly, one of the men broke from the group and tried to circle back toward the River Road. Gallagher hit the gas and raced up the riverbed in hot pursuit.

The Hound gripped the seat. "Careful, Chompo."

He was closing in on the runner, when the man tripped and fell. The ATV hit with a thud, bounced in the air, and came to a halt. The Hound held his head in his hands.

"Holy shit. What have you done now?"

He got out of the ATV and approached the man, who lay groaning on the ground. He aimed a flashlight. Blood was coming out of the man's mouth.

"Gallagher, you stupid son of a bitch."

He went back to the ATV and got on the radio. "Headquarters, this is the Blood Hound. We have a problem."

The next day, Gallagher was thrown out of the West Texas Border Brigade. He was also ordered off the Weaver Ranch. He packed up his trailer and headed west on the River Road.

|Sixteen|

In the morning, Janey dressed and followed the path through the beaten down grass toward the kitchen. Halfway there, she encountered Janko sitting on his sleeping bag. It seemed as if he positioned himself where she was sure to pass.

"Did you sleep well?" he asked.

"I sleep like a baby out here. And you?"

"Yes, I slept well."

"You're not worried about snakes out here?"

"Most creatures won't bother you if you leave them alone. Only humans do that."

That was a little too heavy for 8 am. "I'm on my way to coffee," she said

Janko waved his arm, as if granting her permission to pass. He was clearly frustrated with her lack of communication, but she wasn't comfortable with him. Not after his explosion at Archie.

In the kitchen, she reveled in Robbie's custom-made Canyon Latte, a mixture of coffee and hot chocolate. This was followed by a breakfast of oatmeal mixed with raisins. It was a heavier meal than she was used to, but Robbie assured her she would need the extra calories on the river.

"We've got a long day ahead of us," he said to the

group. "We'll be running four major rapids today, the first about two miles down. After that one, we're going to take a swim at some hot springs."

The words "four major rapids" got her stomach going. Then, Robbie announced he was changing up canoeing partners.

"Lara, you come with me. Peter, you paddle with Richard. Parker, go with Archie. Janey, go with Janko."

She glanced at the Croat. He gave her a wink, as if to say, "you can't avoid me forever."

She went off to take her bathroom break, then helped Lara take down the tent.

"You're with Robbie today," she said. "I'm jealous."

"Janko's nice," Lara answered. "He's a good canoer."

"Yes, he can steer a canoe. I guess I'm lucky he didn't put me with Pooh Bear."

"Poor Pooh Bear. Nobody wants to be stuck with him."

Janey carried her duffel bag down to the shore. Janko waited by his canoe.

"I trust you want me in the bow," she said.

"I think that would be wise."

"I'm nervous about these rapids."

"We'll be fine."

They set out on the river, she enjoying the unhindered view from the bow. It was yet another cloudless day with cool morning temperatures. She never tired of scanning the canyon walls for falcons, hawks, and eagles. And there was always the faint hope of catching a mountain lion unawares, though as Robbie said, they were more likely to be watching her from some invisible perch.

"I'm looking forward to the hot springs," she said. "I don't think I've ever gone three days without a shower or a bath."

"I stink, too."

They paddled on.

"You are alone now," he said.

"You mean in my marriage?"

"Yes."

"That's true. Of course, I have Lara for another few years."

"She's a good kid."

"You pay a lot of attention to her. I think she enjoys that."

"If I had a daughter, she's the kind I'd want."

Janey laughed. "Be careful what you ask for."

She went on to inquire about his family. He said he had none, and she left it at that.

"Are you enjoying being away from your husband?" he said.

"God, yes. Worth would never have signed up for this trip. He would have gone to some beach resort and sat there doing work."

She drank in the scenery, the pineapple-like agave plants clinging to the ledges, the Spanish Daggers standing like soldiers on the grassy slopes below the cliffs. She watched Robbie and Lara paddling just ahead. Robbie seemed to put no effort into his stroke, yet he always stayed ahead. She leaned forward, placing her paddle well to the front and drawing it back hard. Still, they gained no ground.

"Has anyone told you have a nice tush?" Janko said.

She wasn't sure that she'd heard him correctly. Could he have mispronounced another word? No, "tush" is what he said.

"I can tell who's not watching the scenery," she said.

"You American women take offense too easily. You should enjoy the compliment."

She chose not to continue the conversation. Now, she was aware with every stroke, that he was watching her behind. What if *he* were in the bow and she said something about his ass? He'd probably like it. Fucking men.

Robbie slowed and turned to face the group. "This is Hot Springs Rapid coming up, a Class III," he said. "The channel is full of boulders that have washed out from San Rocendo Canyon. We're going to scout it from the Mexican side."

They pulled to the shore and walked down to the head of the rapid. The roar of the water was unnerving—a life-crushing force if you got caught in the wrong place. With all the boulders, the rapid looked nearly impassable, but Robbie pointed out an open passage along the far side of the river.

"You'll see a big slanting rock on the shore," he said. "You want to steer to the right of that and down through a set of big waves. You need to hit those waves straight on, or you'll capsize. If anyone doesn't feel comfortable running this rapid, I can paddle your canoe for you."

She was sorely tempted to say yes, but she was here to challenge herself. She was not going to give in to fear.

They walked back to the boats and tucked themselves into the seats. She worried about her feet getting stuck under the seat if they tipped over. She slid them forward to make sure they didn't catch.

"Alright," she said. "I'm ready."

"Hold on," Janko said. "Give Robbie some space."

When Robbie was halfway down, Janko and Janey

pushed off shore and worked their way across the river and between a line of boulders. There was the big slanting rock, just as Robbie had said. Below it, the river dropped out of sight. Her heart leapt into her mouth as they plunged downward. For a moment, the boat stalled and water poured over the bow.

"Paddle!" Janko yelled.

His command raised her hackles, but she dug in and the canoe broke free of the wave. They glided down to where Robbie and Lara waited in an eddy. Janko gave the command to eddy out. With the canoe half full of water, she was hesitant to lean out and do a draw. She reached gingerly to one side and pulled the bow into the slow water. The stern, still in the current, swung around so fast she was sure they were going to tip over. But Janko kept it steady. They pulled up next to Robbie and Lara.

"Good job," Robbie said. "You both did well to keep your balance."

She felt like a child being praised by a teacher. But she did what he said and it worked. Goddamn, it worked!

They watched the others come though the wave— Richard and Pooh Bear followed by Archie and Parker. They arrived with their canoes full of water.

"Bring your canoes over to the bank and tip them over," Robbie said. "We'll walk down to the hot springs."

There were two springs, each separated from the other by a dozen brushy yards. They were roughly the size of a baby pool, clear with a pebbly bottom. Robbie said they could wear swim suits or go naked, as he preferred.

"We'll make the uppermost spring for the ladies and this one for the men," he said. "Skirts up, pants down, they say on the river."

Janey, Lara, and Parker walked back to the upper spring. Parker went to her canoe to get her bathing suit. "No one wants to see this frumpy body," she said.

Janey and Lara opted to go au naturel. She stepped out of her paddling pants, quick-dry polyester shirt, and underwear and draped them on a creosote bush. She tiptoed across the hard surface and into the water. It was a glorious 85 degrees, as advertised. She sat down, letting the warmth sink in, then leaned back and extended her legs to the sun.

"Oh, this is fantastic," she said.

Lara undressed and stood at the edge of the spring. Her hips had flared out in the past year and her breasts had developed a lovely upward curve. She had shaved her pubic hair, presumably out of deference to the boys that she was dating. Janey was bothered at the thought of her 15-year-old daughter having any manner of sex. At the same time, she was jealous. She'd been celibate for over a year and wondered, at age 42, if she would ever have sex again.

Lara stepped in and moved to the opposite side.

"How was paddling with Robbie?" Janey asked.

"Fine. He's nice."

"What did you two talk about?"

"Stuff."

They floated at opposite sides of the spring, toes touching.

"What did you and Janko talk about?" Lara said.

"I'd rather not say."

"Come on."

"He said I had a nice tush."

"He said that? When?"

"Just out of the blue. While we were paddling."

"Well, it's true, Mom."

She shook her head. "It just makes me wonder what he's thinking."

"Really! It's what all guys are thinking."

Not all guys. Not Worth. She couldn't remember the last time he'd complimented her on her figure. No doubt, her thickening middle was one of the reasons he'd lost interest in her. Fuck him.

Parker arrived and stepped into the pool. The three of them floated on their backs, staring up at the imposing peak across the way.

"Is there a better life than this?" Parker said.

"We are very lucky," Janey said. "Who else knows about this place?"

All too soon, Robbie called from the next spring over that it was time to move on. Janey toweled herself dry and dressed. Walking back toward the canoes, she found Janko staring through a pair of binoculars at the mountain.

"Looking for birds?" she said.

"No, people."

She froze. "There are people up there?"

"I didn't see any. But if I was going to spy on someone that's where I'd be."

She shook her head. "You certainly are suspicious."

Back on the river, the canyon walls rose ever higher. On a dark, rainy day, they would feel oppressive, but on this "bluebird sky" day, the finely-etched walls colored by soft winter light, the scene was a Luminist painting come to life. All that was missing was a noble savage tucked in the corner.

At a bend in the river, the layered rock beneath the

vertical cliffs arched crazily upward, a formation known as the Bullis Fold. Robbie described this as a classic example of "plastic deformation."

"Under extreme pressure, the crust at the Earth's surface is likely to break, but further underground where temperatures are really hot, it's more likely to bend," he said. "So you know that section of earth used to be way down."

Worth used to say that expertise is a turn on, and Janey began to feel that way toward Robbie. It was clear that he'd done a lot of research for the benefit of his clients. It made what could be a desolate landscape so much more interesting.

Beneath the Bullis Fold came another rapid.

"Watch out for the crosscurrents," Robbie yelled.

Bouncing through a series of big waves, Janey's canoe jerked sideways, as if a giant hand were grabbing the bottom of the boat. She grabbed the gunwales, the canoe tipping perilously to one side. Robbie had been watching from the bottom of the rapid.

"Don't ever grab the gunwales," he said, as they pulled up beside him. "You'll pull the canoe right over. If you feel a crosscurrent hit the boat, lean downstream. Show the current the bottom of your canoe."

Janko smiled. "That's what I've been trying to tell her."

"Stop," she said.

Robbie looked at her for an explanation. She would tell him later.

They continued downstream, coursing smoothly around the boulders of Palmas Rapid and through the big waves at Rodeo Rapid. She could feel the power of Janko's stroke. In the still water below Rodeo, she spoke over her shoulder.

"Where did you learn to canoe?" she said.

"We have rivers in Serbia. The Ibar is quite challenging."

"I thought you were from Croatia?

"There are good rivers in both."

High up on a cliff, a bird shot out from its perch, grey speckled wings held straight. "A peregrine falcon!" she said.

Robbie looked up. "You're right. Good eyes."

He called back to the rest of the group. "Janey just spotted a peregrine falcon. That bird was almost extinct a few decades ago."

She appreciated his praise. Other guides seemed to be so full of themselves, eager to expound on everything they knew about a subject. Robbie not only listened to what his clients said, he made sure the others learned about it.

On towards late afternoon, her energy began to flag. The oatmeal and raisins were wearing off. Robbie had warned there would be a difficult rapid at the end of the day and she had been growing steadily more nervous about it. A distant roar announced its arrival. Robbie waved the boats ashore.

Upper Madison Falls was simply too complicated to digest. Sharp-edged rocks jammed the turbulent channel as far as the eye could see. If you flipped your boat here, you could get seriously hurt. The water was too swift to wade and too rocky to float. Robbie announced that it was best to portage the boats to the bottom of the rapid.

"We're going to be camping at the bottom, so just un-load your gear and carry it down."

"What are you going to do?" Archie said.

"I plan to run it. Is there anyone who'd like to go with me?"

Lara immediately raised her hand.

Janey intervened. "No, Lara, it's too dangerous."

"Mom, it's not up to you."

Robbie hesitated, his gaze ending on hers. "Lara, you'd better skip this one."

"God! My one chance."

"I'm sorry. There'll be more rapids."

Janko stepped forward. "I'll run it with you. Do you want me in the stern?"

It was the obvious position for Janko. He was taller and heavier than Robbie. But the guide was not about to relinquish his position of authority.

"We can shift some of the gear toward the back so you don't weigh us down in the bow."

"Whatever you say."

While the two men set about rearranging gear, Janey and the others unloaded their canoes. She and Lara carried her canoe along the long portage trail, Lara rolling her eyes every time she asked to stop for a rest.

On the way back, the whole group stopped to watch Robbie and Janko run the rapid. They started in on the near side, then worked their way to the middle. Bearing down on a pile of boulders, Robbie called out an order. Janko hesitated. Robbie yelled. "Paddle, Dagic!"

Janey was surprised at the harshness in Robbie's voice. The others heard it, too. They were all silent as the two men pulled into the eddy beside the trail.

"You look like a couple of pros," Richard said.

Robbie seemed not to hear. "Janko, you can't hesitate like that in the middle of a rapid."

Janko turned around, meeting Robbie's urgency with equal calm. "Yes, I heard you."

|Seventeen|

The day the group was to run Hot Springs Rapid, Ducharme felt inexplicably down. He stood by the river methodically loading his canoe, when Lara approached with her duffel bag. The prospect of having her with him in the boat lifted his spirits.

"Ahoy, lassie," he said in his pirate voice. "Time to batten down the hatches."

Lara stared at him. "What did you just say?"

"Oh, nothing. It's the way I used to talk in my old job. Go ahead and load your gear."

While Lara tied in her duffel bag, he studied the topo map covering the day's run. A few miles down, Dagger Mountain would come into view on the Texas side. Where the river curved around the base of the mountain, the hot springs should appear on the opposite bank.

"What are you doing?" Lara asked.

"Looking at a map."

"On paper?"

It took him a moment to understand her confusion. "There's no Wifi down here," he said. "Electronics are worthless."

Lara blushed. "Oh, yeah. I forgot."

He folded the map and put it back in its case. "O.K.,

let's go. We're out in front."

It was another blue sky morning, not a breath of wind. The December light was low and soft, giving the landscape a buttery complexion. He had to remind himself that this was winter, the rest of the country covered in snow or drab shades of grey. It felt like cheating somehow, to be out on the river in T-shirts and shorts, the water at your fingertips warm to the touch.

Lara paddled in the same lackadaisical fashion as she did with her mother. She had a swimmer's broad shoulders and muscular arms, so she clearly had the strength to do better. He decided it was time to intervene.

"Lean forward to plant your paddle and bring yourself upright at the end of the stroke," he said. "That engages your back and abdominal muscles instead of just your arms."

Lara did as he suggested. The boat picked up speed.

"I read on your application that you're a swimmer. What's your event?"

"*Was* a swimmer. I quit."

"When'd you do that?"

"Last week."

"Why? I understand you were quite good."

She shrugged. They paddled awhile in silence.

"I hear your parents are in the midst of a divorce," he said. "How's that been on you?"

"It sucks."

"Did that have something to do with your quitting swimming?"

"It just wasn't doing it for me anymore. I mean, I used to really push myself, 'cause I thought if I won it would make things better between my parents. They would smile and everything when I won a race, but it lasted like a second. You could totally tell that they hated their lives."

"So you stopped trying?"

"Yeah, I mean, what for? When they split up, they wouldn't even sit on the same side of the pool, so I had to decide at the end of a meet which one to go to first. Then, the other one would get pissed off. So, I just quit."

"Huh. Well, I hope you find this trip more fun. I know it must be hard with all these adults."

"I kind of don't know how to fit in," she said. "I don't have much to contribute to the conversations."

"You're doing your part just paddling the canoe and helping around the campsite. But I'll try to think of other ways you can contribute."

Arriving at the head of Hot Springs Rapid, he directed everyone to shore. He wouldn't even bother scouting this rapid on the Chattooga—it was just a jag between a few boulders, then a straight shot through a big wave—but he couldn't afford to have someone pin a canoe in the Lower Canyons. Every boat carried essential gear, and there was no room to carry an extra paddler, much less two. He described the route through the rapid, asking Lara in particular if she had any questions.

"Not really," she said.

"O.K., let's do it."

As they approached the line of boulders at the top of the rapid, he called on Lara to execute a left-side draw. She reached her paddle out to the side and pulled the bow hard to the left. Lined up perfectly, they plunged through the big wave. Lara raised her arms overhead and let out a whoop. All this girl needed was a challenge.

As the boaters paddled to shore at the base of the rapid,

Ducharme led them over to the hot springs. He designated one for the women and one for the men, telling them they could wear swim suits or go naked, as was his preference.

When the ladies had left, he stripped down and eased himself into the water. Richard and Archie did the same, followed by Peter and Dagic. Richard and Archie had typical physiques for 50-something men—some muscle tone in their arms, a gut coming on. But the difference between Peter and Dagic was striking. Peter was a pink-skinned, hairless man, with a smooth chest and a nub for a penis. When he floated on his back, his belly protruded a good three inches above the surface. Dagic was cut like an athlete, with a hairy chest and big, swinging dick.

While the others basked in the spring with eyes unfocused, Dagic surveyed his surroundings. "What do they call that mountain across the river?" he said.

"That's Dagger Mountain, also known as Lomas de las Palmas," Ducharme said.

"Is there a trail up there?"

"There is, but it's a tough climb. I've heard that immigrants use it as a way to get on top of the rim and over to Sanderson."

"There are immigrants way out here?"

"Some. With all the increased surveillance, people are being forced to cross in more remote areas. There's not a paved road within a hundred miles of the border on the Mexican side. On this side, it's at least 30 miles. You'd have to be really desperate to want to cross here."

Dagic got dressed and swaggered off through the brush. Archie watched him go. "That's what's called being hung like a horse," he said.

Ducharme laughed. Penises never ceased to be a

source of interest for men, even when the days of locker room competition were long gone.

"O.K., folks," he said. "Time to get moving."

He dressed and walked back to his canoe. Lara arrived wearing a wry smile.

"What?" he said.

"Nothing. Just something my mom said."

Obviously, there'd been a conversation in the ladies' room about sex. Had they caught a glimpse of Dagic?

Back on the river, he resumed his questioning about Lara's relationship with her mother. Did they get along?

"She's just in a bad mood so much of the time," Lara said.

"She seems to be enjoying this trip."

"Yeah, she likes this stuff. My Dad doesn't do adventure."

"Is that why they split up?"

"Partly, I guess. Once me and my sister grew up, Mom saw how life was going to be and she didn't like it."

He reflected on that statement. Carmen had seen how their life was going to be. Him struggling to make a living on the river. Maybe calling it quits. You couldn't blame someone for being afraid.

"Do you have a girlfriend?" Lara asked.

"I hope so. It's been on-again off-again of late."

He told her the story of the dog getting run over, of Carmen's asking him to leave.

"That's awful. Maybe she'll forgive you."

"I think she has, but that doesn't mean she'll accept me as her partner. There are things about me that she doesn't care for."

Lara looked over her shoulder and gave him a tender

smile.

"Well, I hope you find someone."

|Eighteen|

Ducharme opened his eyes to the inner hull of his canoe. He turned in his sleeping bag and stared up at the chalk blue sky between the cliffs. If only his universe was contained within these walls. There would be no sadness, no confusion. He would rise with the dawn and cook breakfast, call his sleepy clients from their tents. They would sip their coffee and speak of the day to come. Then, they would board their canoes and venture forth on the Rio Grande.

Maybe someday he would find a woman to join him on the river. They would watch the light etch the stony walls and listen to the song of the canyon wren. They would paddle through the stillness of the morning, ever watchful for the deer, the big horn sheep, the javelina come down to the river to drink.

At mid-day, they would bathe naked in the hot springs and nap in the shade of the yellow-flowering mesquite. They would rise again in the afternoon and paddle until the canyon walls turned crimson, and a campsite beck- oned on a grassy shore. He would cook dinner, fill the air with the smell of curried chicken. As darkness fell, they would lay on their backs and watch the satellites cross the sky in never-ending orbits. They, too, would always have one more turn, one more bend in the river. They would be forever young, forever in love, forever in the thrall of the Lower Canyons.

A groaning noise rose from the campsite, followed by a second and a third. He sat up to find the realtors—Parker, Archie, Richard, and Peter—emerging from their tents. They lurched forward on stiff limbs, arms out to their sides. Zombies. They wandered in circles at first, then turned toward him. Janey and Lara stuck their heads out of their tent, grinning with anticipation. The zombies converged on the canoe, grabbed at his arms and shoulders. He feigned a howl of pain, and the scene devolved into laughter.

"Okay, you zombies," he said. "Turn me loose if you want coffee."

He dressed and started the water boiling. On this trip, he'd developed a new flavor he called Mocha Robbie, combining two parts coffee and one part hot chocolate. The group stood in line for that.

"Zombie like Mocha Robbie," Archie said.

Ducharme pointed to the mountain across the river. "Today, you zombies are going to climb Burro Bluff," he said. "It's a thousand feet up, but there's a good trail and the view is not to be missed. Bring your cameras."

After breakfast, the group ferried their canoes across the river and started up the switchbacked path between the prickly pear cactus. Dagic strode ahead of the others, his long legs gobbling a yard at a time. Ducharme picked up the rear, Parker moving slowly ahead of him. With each bend in the trail, the gap between them and the other hikers grew.

Halfway up, Ducharme called for a water break. Parker collapsed on a nearby rock, her armpits bathed in sweat.

A shout rang out from the top of the bluff. Dagic.

"I can't believe he's already up there," Janey said.

Archie sniffed. "Where's an avalanche when we need one."

The realtors laughed. It was disheartening for Ducharme to see a schism developing in the group, though he couldn't blame them. Dagic was bent on keeping himself apart.

"Let's move on," he said.

Archie and Janey got to their feet, but Parker shook her head.

"These hips aren't made for walking," she said. "I think I'll stay here."

He frowned. "Don't give up yet. The view from the top is totally worth it."

When he was a boy, Ducharme resisted being dragged on hikes by his parents. He sometimes stopped in the middle of a trail and refused to go on. His father would practice a diversionary tactic, asking him to talk about what he wanted to wear for Halloween, what he wanted for Christmas. It would always get him going again.

"Parker, how about telling me about your children," he said, "We can walk while you talk."

She got to her feet. "Well, my daughter's getting married in the spring."

"Nice. Who's going to be coming to the wedding?"

"Oh, let's see..."

Twenty minutes later, they reached the top of the bluff. Janey gave Parker a hug. "You did it, girl!"

They tiptoed to the rim where the bluff dropped a thousand feet straight down to the Rio Grande. From here, the river appeared as a muddy ribbon winding between chalky cliffs. The surface was smooth all the way to Upper Madison Falls, a maze of boulders and churning rapids.

"You can see the rock we almost hit, Janko," Ducharme said. "Right there at the bottom of the rapid."

"I see it."

On both sides of the river, the dry, mountainous landscape spread in endless folds, not a building or road in sight.

"You say it's 50 miles to the nearest road?" Dagic said.

"Something like that."

"We'd die if we had to hike out," Richard said.

Lara spoke. "I bet I could do it."

Ducharme smiled. "Really? Fifty miles? It's not straight. It's up and down through all kinds of cactus. And there's no water. I tell people if you have to get out, the only way is down the river."

"I still think I could do it."

As the heat of mid-day came on, he led the group down the bluff and back to camp. People retreated to their tents to nap. He took this rare opportunity to be alone.

Behind the campsite, a faint path led into a narrow cleft in the canyon wall. He wound his way through the boulders and found a patch of shade beneath a honey mesquite tree. He sat on the sandy ground and leaned against the trunk. With the trip more than half over, he found himself thinking of home. His relationship with Carmen remained painfully unresolved. His undependability had been revealed, and together with the tenuousness of his business, she was unlikely to make any commitment. And there was this other thing always lingering in the back of his mind. The thing on the Chattooga...

A figure approached—Janey.

"There you are," she said. "I was wondering where you'd gone."

She came within half-a-dozen feet and stopped.

"You decided to take a break from the group?"

"Yes," he said.

"Do you want to be alone?"

"That's alright. Have a seat."

"You look a bit tired," she said.

"I was just thinking of all the things I need to do back home."

"Where is it that you live?"

"Aintry. It's a small town a couple of hours north."

"And you live by yourself?"

He nodded.

"You were wonderful with Parker this morning," she said. "I can't believe you got her to go to the top."

"She just needed some encouragement."

Janey smiled, brushed back the hair on the side of her face. She was a beautiful woman, older than he was normally attracted to, but beautiful nonetheless.

"So, you have another daughter?" he said.

"Yes. Anna. She's two years older than Lara."

"And she's moved in with your husband?"

"My ex-husband. I'm the unreasonable mother. Worth has convinced her of that."

"He sounds like a real asshole."

"I'm lucky to still have Lara. He hasn't been able to completely win her over. Yet." She was silent for a time. "I take it you don't have children."

"No. Never been married."

"In love with the rivers, huh?"

He smiled. "They're not everything."

"Well, you've saved yourself some heartache by staying single."

His mood sinking at the thought, he changed the subject. "So, what was that exchange between you and Janko?"

She rolled her eyes. "He was making an analogy between your recommendation to turn the bottom of the canoe toward the current to his desire for me to show off my ass."

"Really? Do I have to speak to him about that?"

"No, it's alright. I imagine you already talked to him about snapping at Archie. I don't want him to feel like a pariah."

"You let me know if it becomes a problem."

She nodded. "I guess managing your clients' interpersonal relations is as difficult as teaching them to run the rapids."

"It can be."

"You're very good at it."

"Not always."

"You're being modest."

The image of Maria crept back in his mind. Tears welled in his eyes.

"What?" she said.

"It's nothing."

She got up and put her hands on his face, searched his eyes for an answer. "Tell me what happened?"

His heart beat fast. He wanted to speak, to tell her everything. She of all people would understand. But he had to resist. He was the guide. He had to remain aloof.

"We should get back," he said.

|Nineteen|

The first thing Gallagher did after his firing was to drive to Porter's Thriftway in Presidio and buy a Styrofoam cooler, two bags of ice and a case of beer.

The young Hispanic woman at the checkout counter smiled at Gallagher. "Ola."

"This is America, sweetheart," he said. "No habla Español."

"I'm so sorry," she said.

"I'll forgive you this time."

The drive-in sites at The Hoodoos Campground were nearly full. Children played in the gravel next to the RVs, adults manned barbecues. He found one last spot near the river, backed in the Airstream. He hooked up the electrical, unrolled the awning, set a lawn chair underneath and popped open the first beer.

Down the hill, the Rio Grande chattered over the rocks. It was as happy a sound as he'd ever known. He opened a second beer and started to sing. "*Mommas, don't let your babies grow up to be cowboys...*"

As the sun went down, he sang louder. A man appeared at his side.

"Sir, would you mind keeping it down? We're trying to put our children to bed."

"Sure, sure, I'll keep it down." Fuck head.

He cracked open a third beer. Darkness came on and an orange moon rose over the river. Spectacular! He broke into Creedence' song "Bad Moon Rising."

The man returned. "Sir, if you don't quiet down, I'm going to have to call the ranger."

"The fuck, you say."

"Sir, I'm going to call the ranger right now."

He sat up, his head spinning. "Don't call the ranger. I'll take my ass down to the river if that's what you want."

He gathered up a handful of beer and stumbled down the trail. Screw the neighbors. Screw everybody. He looked up to see a hoodoo silhouetted against the night sky, its giant "head" balanced atop its torso.

"Good evening to you, sir," he said.

He wobbled, then collapsed in the trail.

Some time later, he awoke to feel a boot poking his ribs. He opened his eyes to see four men standing above him in the dark. They conversed in Spanish.

"Es ese el hombre que nos persiguio?"

"Si, ese es el."

Mexicans. He struggled to a sitting position. "Que pasa, amigos?"

The men's pants were wet. They had just waded across the river.

"Aren't you the guy who lived in the silver trailer up on the hill?" one of them said.

Gallagher's head swam. How did they know him?

"The guy who chased us the other night on your ATV?" another said. "You ran down our friend. You broke his back. The doctors say he may never walk again."

He cleared his throat. "I was just doing my job. If you

boys stayed on your side of the river, there wouldn't be any trouble."

The men frowned. "Que haremos con el?"

"Tomemos su ropa."

At that, one man stepped forward and pinned Gallagher's hands over his head. Another held his legs. He yelled and squirmed as they stripped him and kicked him in the ribs.

"Adios, pendejo. Don't let your white ass get sunburned."

They disappeared up the hill.

He struggled to stand. "You bastards! Get back here with my clothes!" He fell over in the dirt and passed out again.

Some hours later, he woke to find the sun in his face. He sat up, nursed his sore ribs. Motherfuckers. He looked for his clothes, found only his hat. He stood up and wiped the pebbles off his ass.

Getting his bearings, he tip-toed back to the campground, covering his genitals with his hat. Fortunately, no one else was up. He pulled on the Airstream door. Locked!

He approached the trailer next to his and knocked on the door. A little girl answered.

"Excuse me, miss, is your daddy there?"

She screamed. A woman came to the door, gasped and slammed it in his face.

"Hey, I just need some pants. I got robbed!"

A man's voice rang out. "Stay the hell away from here, buddy!"

As Gallagher was walking to the next trailer, a park ranger sped into the campground. He skidded to a halt and stepped out with his hand on his holster.

"Stay right where you are," the ranger said. "Put your hands on your head."

"You sure you want me to do that?"

He set his hat on his head. The ranger winced.

"Alright, put 'em down. What are you doing without your clothes?"

"I got jumped by illegals down by the river. They took my clothes and locked me out of my trailer."

The ranger stared. "Your name's Gallagher, right? You were parked here most of the summer."

"That's me."

"Get inside my vehicle. We're going for a ride."

He climbed into the front seat and put his hat in his lap, happy to be out of the public eye.

"You taking me to get some clothes?" he said.

The ranger steered out of the campground headed west. "I'm taking you to Presidio. This is a police matter."

"Aw, don't take me to Taco Town. They'll crucify me over there."

"Sir, that is not my problem."

|Twenty|

When she and Kelin walked into the migrant shelter in the heart of Oaxaca, Sayda expected to be treated like dirt. At the bus station, the first person she'd asked about a place to stay had scowled at her.

"Go back to Honduras," the woman said. "We don't need you here."

The next woman was a bit kinder. She, too, frowned, but told them about the shelter. She and Kelin roamed the streets of the strange city, asking for directions. Finally, they found it on a side street, surrounded by a wall enclosing a courtyard with trees.

The woman who greeted them smiled. "Come in," she said. "Where are you traveling from?"

Her expression didn't change when she said Honduras. The woman seated behind the desk smiled as well.

"You're just in time for lunch," she said.

"How much does it cost?" Sayda asked.

"There's no charge. You can also sleep here for free. We have mats and blankets. If you need medical help, we have a nurse on staff. Just let me know."

She fought back tears. This was the first person who'd been kind to them the entire trip, the first person who'd offered hope. She and Kelin collected their mats and blankets and headed to the "dormitory," a large empty room save for people scattered around the floor, looking at cell phones, sleeping, reading.

The first thing she did after unrolling her mat was take off her shoes and socks. She hadn't done this in a week.

"God, my feet stink," she said.

Kelin turned up his nose. "Guacala! They smell like rancid onions."

A boy sitting on his mat a few yards away overheard. "You can give your clothes to the lady up front," he said. "They'll wash them."

She thanked him, but said nothing else. How embarrassing to have a cool-looking stranger smell your feet.

The cafeteria was filled with young people and a scattering of adults. Sayda sat next to a desultory looking girl about her age. She introduced herself, discovered that Emely was also from Honduras.

"Are you traveling alone?" Sayda asked.

"No, I'm with my parents." Emely nodded to a man and a woman sitting in the corner.

Sayda sensed there was some reason for their separation. Families almost always sat together.

"Are you traveling north?" she asked.

Emely shook her head. "We're being deported."

"By whom?"

"First by the U.S. We got caught crossing the river. Now, Mexico is deporting us back to Honduras."

"Why?"

Emely shrugged. "My father says the Americans are paying the Mexicans."

Her heart sank. This was not something she'd been warned about.

"What'll happen when you return home?"

Emely looked toward her parents, but said nothing.

"The gangs killed my father and threatened my brother," Sayda said. "I could never go back."

"I think they will kill my father, too," Emely said.

After lunch, Sayda went outside and called her mother, told her they'd arrived safely in Oaxaca. Her mother was heartened, but when she heard her daughter's account of the girl being deported by Mexico, she began to cry.

"You may be alright, but Kelin must not come back," she said. "A gang member came by the store looking for him. Don't tell him that. I don't want him to worry, but you must not bring him back."

She, too, began to cry. "What are we supposed to do?"

"You have to get across the border. Show the authorities the newspaper article. Tell them the situation."

That evening, Kelin told her that he'd talked to the boy who was sitting near them in the dormitory. His name was Daniel and he had plans for making it to the border.

"He tried to go by bus, but got turned back," Kelin said. "He says he knows of a train we could sneak onto."

She shook her head. "Grandfather said not to take the trains. The railroad guards will catch us."

"He said he knows a way. Let's talk to him at dinner."

Daniel was a handsome boy with soft eyes and a ready smile, not like so many others who seemed beaten down by their journey.

"You must be twins," he said as they sat down together at the table. "Which one of you is the smartest?"

Kelin gave a bashful smile. "She is."

"The best looking, too."

Over a meal of rice and beans, Daniel talked of his plans to jump a train outside of town. "You can't jump them in the yards anymore. The guards will catch you. And you can't ride on top where they can see you. But if you can get on a hopper car after the train has left the yard, you have a chance. You'll at least get to Mexico City."

She frowned. "It sounds dangerous."

Daniel shrugged. "What are you going to do? They stop all the buses going north. They'll throw you off for sure."

"What about asking a truck driver?" Kelin said.

"They won't take you. They can lose their commercial driver's license if they get caught transporting illegals. You should come with me. I know we can make it."

She glanced at Kelin. "Maybe we will."

That night, the three of them lay side by side on their mats. The lights were off, but she could see Daniel's form on the other side of Kelin. She closed her eyes for awhile. When she opened them, Daniel was looking right at her. He didn't blink, didn't look away. He was in love with her.

The next morning, the three of them ate their breakfast and said goodbye to the staff.

"How do you plan to travel?" one of the staff members asked.

"We've got a ride," Daniel said.

The staffer looked skeptical. "Whatever you do, please be careful."

They walked for hours along the Oaxaca-Tehuantepec Highway leading out of town. Several miles along, Sayda noticed a big warehouse by the side of the road with at least a dozen long-haul trucks pulled up to the bays.

"Look at all those trucks," she said. "Don't you think

we should ask one of the drivers for a lift?"

"Forget it," Daniel said. "Unless you offer to screw one of them, you won't stand a chance."

Kelin snorted. "Fat chance. She's still a virgin."

"Shut up, Kelin. What would you know?"

As the sun was sinking low, a line of railroad cars loomed on the horizon.

"That's the yard," Daniel said. "We have to go beyond that."

They left the highway and crossed a field of corn stubble.

"We wait here," Daniel said. "Stay out of sight until the engine passes, then look for a hopper. They're the ones with the slanted fronts."

She lay in the weeds amidst the steady trill of the crickets. Night was coming, the yellow glow in the western sky fading to blue.

Kelin saw the headlight first. "There's an engine!"

"It's not moving," she said. Then, she heard the thrum of the engine.

"It's coming," Daniel said. "Stay down."

The bright red engine came slowly. She thought it would be easy to jump on board, but as the cars passed, she realized that even a slow moving train was going faster than most people could run.

The first group was all box cars, but then came the open-topped hoppers. Daniel jumped up. "Come on."

It was hard running on the gravel. The stones wobbled beneath her feet, sapping her speed. Daniel reached the ladder of the second car, grabbed it and hoisted himself up onto the platform. Sayda's soccer muscles kicked in.

"Come on!" Daniel yelled. "Grab the rung!"

She felt herself lifted off the ground. Her shoes dragged across the gravel, but with help from Daniel, she pulled herself up onto the platform. Kelin was running right behind, but the train was gaining speed. She shouted encouragement. He reached for the ladder, but lost his grip. He fell with his arm outstretched, screamed in pain and rolled down the embankment.

She yelled. "He's hurt!"

"Don't worry, he'll get the next train," Daniel said.

She watched her brother rise to his knees and raise the stub of an arm. She turned and kissed Daniel on the lips.

"I love you," she said, and leapt off the train.

$$***$$

When Kelin emerged from Oaxaca's Hospital del Valle Emergencia, his left arm was covered in white bandages where his hand used to be. Sayda burst into tears, ran up and hugged him.

Kelin cried, too. "I'm so sorry, Sayda. I couldn't hold on."

"Don't worry," she said. "You can still play soccer."

Kelin looked at his sister. "You're hurt, too."

When Sayda had jumped off the train, she was thrown face first onto the gravel. The tip of her nose and lips were scraped bare, along with the palms of her hands. The doctors had coated them with antibiotics, but that was all they could do.

"What do we do, now?" Kelin asked.

"Let's go back to the shelter. We'll figure it out from there."

The staff at the shelter were heartbroken. "We warned

you about that train," they said.

Sayda and Kelin retreated to the dorm and slumped against the wall.

"Maybe we should go back home," Kelin said. "The gangs won't want me with just one hand."

She shook her head. "We're not going back."

Over the coming days, Kelin grew increasingly despondent. A phone call to his mother did nothing to alleviate his sadness. He stopped talking, stared at his stump for hours on end. It took all of the staff's persuasion to get him to eat. Sayda knew she had to get him moving again.

"I want to try one more thing," she said. "If it doesn't work, we'll go home. Do you remember the warehouse we passed with all the trucks in front? I'm going to ask one of the drivers to take us. We still have some money left. Maybe one will say yes."

The next evening, after dinner, they walked back out the Oaxaca-Tehuantepec Highway. It was dark by the time they made it to the warehouse, just as she'd planned. There were still a few trucks backed up to the building, trailer doors open. She and Kelin snuck up to the end of the loading dock.

"You stay out of sight until I call you," she said. "Don't come looking for me. This might take awhile."

Kelin's eyes widened. "What are you going to do?"

"Don't worry."

She approached the first truck. There was no one in the cab. She caught Kelin peaking around the corner of the loading dock and waved him back. Just then, a man came down the stairs from the loading dock. He wore a white cowboy hat, jeans, and boots. He was not as old as her father, maybe 45, she didn't know. He stared at her as he approached his truck.

"Excuse me, sir," Sayda said. "Are you going north?"

He stopped. "Yes, but I don't take riders."

"I can pay you."

She pulled out a wad of pesos. He studied her face. "What happened to you?"

"I fell off the train. My brother fell, too. He lost his hand."

The man sighed. "You kids. Like I told you, I can't take riders. If I'm caught by the authorities, I could lose my job."

She feared it would come to this. The blood rushed to her face. She didn't even know the right words to use.

"Please, sir," she said. "I will offer myself to you."

He stared. "How old are you?"

"Fifteen. Sixteen!"

The man motioned to the cab. "Alright. Get in quick."

He opened the door. She stepped up into the cab. The seats were like lounge chairs, the dashboard a maze of dials and buttons. Taped to the top of the windshield, just above the steering wheel, was a picture of the Virgin Mary.

The man closed the door behind him. "Get in the back. It'll be easier."

In the dark space behind the seats was a raised bed with a mattress, sheets, and a blanket. She crawled onto the bed and sat.

The driver looked at her. "Well?"

She took off her sandals and jeans, started to unbutton her shirt.

"Don't bother with that," he said.

She slipped off her underwear and laid back with her

legs locked together. The driver turned on a light above the bed.

"Let me see you," he said.

She parted her legs.

"Jesus."

He moved between the seats, put one knee on the bed and unbuckled his pants. She looked away, her gaze alighting on the picture of the Virgin Mary. The driver lowered himself on top of her, blocking out the overhead light. She felt the weight of his chest on hers, then his penis pushing against her hymen. She cried out in pain.

He stopped. "Have you ever done this before?"

"No."

He sat back and zipped up his jeans.

"I can do it," she said. "I won't cry."

He shook his head. "Go find your brother. I'll take you to Mexico City."

|Twenty-One|

Janey went back to her tent to find Lara awake, playing some game on her phone.

"Where have you been?" Lara said.

"I was talking with Robbie."

"I thought so."

She lay down on her sleeping bag and took out a book.

"What were you talking about, if I may ask?"

"I was complimenting him on dealing with Parker. You didn't see it, but about halfway up the bluff, she wanted to quit. Robbie talked her into going on by having her think of something else besides the climb."

"You like him, don't you?"

She smiled. "He's pretty cute."

"Don't get any big ideas."

That drew a laugh. She pretended to go back to her book, but, in truth, she was reveling in this exchange with her daughter, something that would never have happened at home. Being physically confined in a tent seemed to induce intimate conversations.

"Do you miss not being able to communicate with your friends?" she said.

Lara sniffed. "Not really."

"Seriously?"

"Yeah. I didn't think that could ever happen."

She mulled that over, thought of the things in her own life that she never imagined, until recently, could happen.

As evening arrived, people came out of their tents and relaxed against the canoe couches. Robbie prepared another one of his special meals—Mexicano Macaroni. Janey watched in admiration as he diced onions, green peppers and tomatoes with a practiced hand—forefinger held under the crook of the knife. He sautéed this mixture and added a couple of cans of something called Rotel, which turned out to be Mexican chilis and tomatoes. He mixed this concoction with macaroni, spooned it into plastic bowls, topped it with salsa and grated cheese, and a piece of pita bread.

"Robbie, why aren't you married?" Archie said. "You're such a good cook. My wife would marry you for that reason alone."

"Thanks, but people aren't exactly lining up to marry someone who's out on the river half the time," he said.

"But you'd get married if you had the chance."

"Sure."

"How about you, Janko?" Archie said.

Janey was surprised to hear Archie engage the man who'd accused him of talking too much. But Janko seemed not to mind.

"I was married once. A long time ago."

"Did you have children?" Parker asked.

"No, it didn't last that long."

"Pooh Bear was married," Archie said.

Peter blushed. "Yes, but Pooh Bear found out he was gay."

Faces lit up around the group.

"How did that end?" Robbie asked.

"We just kind of called the whole thing off."

Archie was on a roll, getting people to talk about themselves. He clearly loved this. "What about you, Janey?" he said. "Are you going to remarry?"

She rolled her eyes. "I'm not ready to think about that."

"Give it at least a year," Parker said. "I was divorced and I got back in too soon. Fortunately, I didn't marry the bastard."

Janey managed a smile. Across the river, an ever-narrowing band of reflected light colored the top of the canyon wall. She put her empty bowl in the dish pan, returned to her tent, and came back with her camera.

"Check that out," Robbie said to the group.

The progress of shadow and light on the canyon walls was like an upside down window shade, Janey thought. The shade lowered from the top down in the morning and raised from the bottom up in the evening. Now, with just the top edge of the cliff gilt in light, she took her photo.

Darkness fell and the stars came out in the narrow band of sky. She'd come to love this nightly show, everyone's attention directed at the infinitude above. There was talk about mind-blowing things—the shape of space, the illusion of time.

"I've heard that it's theoretically possible to travel forward in time, but not backward," Richard said. "You can't change the past."

A long silence followed, everyone lost in their own thoughts. Robbie broke the spell.

"Folks, tomorrow's our last full day on the river," he said. "We'll have three big rapids and a bunch of wall shots."

"How big?" Peter asked.

"Lower Madison Falls is a Class III. It's got a tricky cross current and a big drop. Panther Rapid is a wall shot. I'd rate it a Class II, but if you hit the wall, you're likely to tip over. San Francisco is a III. There are lot of boulders in the channel washed out from San Francisco Canyon and the number and position of them changes every year. Below the boulder field, the current runs into an undercut cliff. You want to stay off of that."

Peter shook his head. "Guess who's going to buy it tomorrow?"

"I'm going to put you with Janko, so you should be fine," Robbie said.

Janko gave a weird smile. He was clearly not pleased with his assignment.

She, too, started feeling butterflies. Was Robbie going to put her with one of the lesser canoeists—Archie or Richard? Was he going to ask her to paddle stern through Class III rapids? She didn't feel up to that.

Clouds appeared and hid the stars. The campsite turned pitch black save for the narrow beams of headlamps. She had yet to clean the dishes and offered to do so.

"I'll help you," Janko said. He got up and began collecting the dishes.

Robbie took the hot water off the stove and poured it into one of the plastic tubs, then squirted in some liquid soap. The other tub he filled with fresh water from a jerry can.

"This is the last of our drinking water, so fill up your bottles before you go to bed," he said. "We'll refill the cans tomorrow at a spring below Lower Madison Falls."

She and Janko carried their tubs down to the river. The night was hot and still. Flying insects swarmed in front of her headlamp as she knelt by the shore.

"I hate these bugs," she said.

Janko shrugged. "They don't seem to bite."

She scraped macaroni off the dishes and into the river.

"I hope this isn't polluting the water."

"I wouldn't worry about it."

She sponged the dishes in the soapy water and handed them to Janko, who rinsed them in the clean water and dried them with a towel.

"How are you feeling about tomorrow?" she said. "The rapids sound pretty challenging."

"I hope Robbie puts me with you," he said. "You're a good canoeist."

"Thank you. We made a good team."

Janko smiled at her, and she immediately regretted the remark.

"I can't believe the trip is almost over," she said.

"Still time for fun."

That was it. She handed him the last of the dishes and stood. "I'm going to turn in," she said.

Janko held her sleeve. "Why don't you stay? Enjoy the evening."

"No, I'm pretty tired."

She pulled away and headed back to the tent, half expecting him to follow.

Lara was already in her sleeping bag. "Did you have a nice time at the river?" she said.

"Ugh. That man gives me the creeps."

"He's hot for you mom."

"Mom is hot, but not for him." She unbuttoned her

shirt and bra, aired out her sweaty breasts. "All mom wants to do is sleep."

But she could not sleep. Not well. She dreamed of being stuck in a canoe with some man she couldn't see who ran the canoe dangerously close to the rocks. She tried to steer the boat away, but no matter how hard she pulled, she couldn't change its direction.

|Twenty-Two|

Ducharme stood before the gathered canoeists. "Lara, I want you to go with Richard, Parker with Archie. Peter, you go with Janko. Janey, you're with me. Lower Madison Falls is just about a mile downstream. We'll pull out on the left to scout it."

He waited for Janey to settle into the bow of the canoe, then took a seat in the stern. He instructed everyone to tighten the straps holding down the equipment and give the sagging airbags a few extra breaths to firm them up.

"And make sure you have your extra paddles and your throw ropes handy," he said. "You don't want that paddle shoved under a bunch of equipment where you can't get at it in a hurry."

He pulled the topographic maps out of the clear plastic bag and found the one that covered Lower Madison Falls. He folded that on top and resealed the bag.

"Alright, let's go."

Janey started paddling, a nice even stroke that was easy to follow.

"Are you excited about today?" he said.

She glanced over her shoulder. "I'm nervous, to tell you the truth. But I'm glad to be with you."

In short order, they reached the head of Lower

Madison Falls. He pulled out on the Texas shore and tied the canoe to a mesquite tree. The others pulled in behind him and together they scaled the bank and walked to the bluff overlooking the falls. The rapid was more of a staircase than a falls, the river plunging over a series of two-foot drops with boulders mixed in between.

He gave his instructions, pointing out the biggest obstacles. "Hug the left shoreline to get past that first set of boulders, then cut back to the right to avoid those others. See them? They're just barely under water."

The others conferred with their partners about what moves to make.

"Janey and I will go first. After we get through the rapid, I'll climb the bank and signal the next boat to come on. Do *not* go unless and until you see me give you the sign."

He and Janey went back to their canoe, pushed off and paddled to midstream. From the low seating position of the canoe, most of the rapid was invisible. He held an image in his head of what he'd seen, but he couldn't be sure of where they were. The roar of falling water filled the air, the horizon line dropped, the canoe rushed forward. He glanced at the boulders as they flew past, working his paddle to keep the boat between them and the shore.

"Draw right!"

Janey dug her paddle in, drawing the bow across the current. They plunged over the drops and glided into smooth water.

"Well done," he said. "Let's eddy out to the right."

"That was exciting!"

He unclipped his throw rope, climbed onto the bank

and signaled the next boat to come on. Richard and Lara appeared. They followed a good line, dodging the boulders then angling across the current. They charged over the last drop and pulled into the eddy.

Janey called out, "Great job, Lara!"

He grabbed the bow as they came to shore, instructing Richard to step out and get his throw rope ready.

Back atop the bluff, he signaled Archie and Parker to come on. From the start, he could see they were in trouble. Archie kept the boat too close to the shore, and by the time they tried to cut back to midstream, it was too late. They hit one of the submerged boulders and capsized.

"Boat over!" he shouted to Richard.

As Parker swept past, Richard tossed his throw bag. Parker grabbed the rope as it hit the water. Richard pulled her in, while Ducharme raced down the bluff. Archie drifted past, holding on to the canoe with one hand and his paddle with the other. He tossed Archie a rope and pulled him and the swamped canoe into the eddy.

"Are you okay?" he said.

"I'm fine. How's Parker?"

His bow partner was bent over, Janey at her side.

"She's okay, but she banged her knee on a rock," Janey said.

He coiled his rope and instructed Richard to do the same. When both men were ready, he signaled Dagic to come on. The Croat entered the rapid on a good line, passing the upstream boulders with room to spare. Peter attempted a draw to get them into midstream, but his stroke was weak and they hit one of the submerged rocks, nearly capsizing the canoe. As they pulled into the eddy, Dagic shook his head in disgust.

Ducharme waited until they were safely grounded, then went to examine Parker's knee.

"Looks like it's just bruised," he said. "I've got a cold pack you can put on it when we get to camp."

He called for the group to take a break while he filled up two jerry cans from the spring.

"Janey, come help me."

While the others sagged in the grass, he and Janey carried the containers downstream to where water trickled down a rocky bank. The ledges protruded just enough that you could set a can underneath and capture the stream of spring water. He knelt down and held his can under one rivulet, Janey the other. It was a slow process.

"This is a good way to calm my jittery nerves," Janey said.

"Did that rapid scare you?"

"Yes. My heart was going wild."

"You know, you have the skills to run any of these rapids," he said. "Your mind can work against you because you see all the places you can screw up. But if you break down each move, none of them are that hard to do."

"Like raising a child," Janey said. "I always worried about all the things that could go wrong."

"Did that distance you from your kids?"

"Probably. It certainly turned Worth off."

He nodded. "I do have to say, I thought at the beginning of this trip that you were going to be a problem."

Janey blanched. "What? Why?"

"You don't remember accosting me at the motel? You said I'd undersold the dangers of the trip and that you might not have come if you'd known that."

"Oh, God, I am so sorry."

"That's O.K. You haven't been any trouble."

She put her hand on his arm. "I hope not."

Now, he was the one who felt nervous. A woman a decade older than him, with life experiences he'd never known, was seeking his approval. Not on canoeing or setting up a tent, but on behaving as an adult.

The water spurted out of the top of the can. "O.K., that's enough," he said.

They closed the tops and lugged the jerry cans back to the canoes. Everyone was looking at them.

"What took you so long?" Archie said.

"Yeah, we thought you'd gone and left us," Parker said.

"It takes awhile to fill a can from a spring," he said.

He stowed the jerry cans in his canoe and briefed the group on the next rapid. Panther Canyon featured a fast, narrow run under an overhanging rock wall. "We'll scout it from the left bank."

Two miles down, they pulled up to a grassy clearing and scaled a twenty-foot-high bluff. From there, they could see where the river bent underneath the cliff.

"Just remember, on the inside of every sharp bend, there's usually an eddy," he said. "Keep to the inside of the bend, but don't run into that eddy. It'll turn your boat back upstream."

He and Janey climbed into their canoe and headed into the rapid. As they fell under the shadow of the overhang, the current picked up speed. White-tipped waves sprouted from the darkness, the rush of the water echoing off the wall. Janey kept the boat moving while he ruddered in the stern, holding the bow just outside the eddy line.

Once in slow water, he turned the boat around and waved the others on. Janey got out her camera and aimed upstream. One by one, the boats raced beneath the cliff and emerged into the sunlight. Seeing Janey with the camera, the canoeists hammed it up. Even Dagic gave a thumb and pinky-fingered salute.

"Good job, everyone," Ducharme said. "We'll take a lunch break about six miles down. There's a nice hike up a side canyon."

San Francisco Creek was a wide, perennially dry stream whose gravelly bed served as a highway for wildlife. Sure enough, as the canoeists approached, a herd of mountain sheep scampered out of the creek and up the brushy sides of the canyon. The group watched until the sheep disappeared over the top of the bluff, then brought their canoes ashore.

While Ducharme prepared lunch, the others explored the surroundings. They found shallow caves at the base of the canyon walls and deep pools of water, tinajas, at the bottom of bowl-like depressions. Richard discovered fossils of ammonites, an extinct form of mollusk, pressed into the rock. Archie called out that he'd found a mountain lion track.

Dagic stayed with Ducharme, eating from a package of dried prunes. "So when does this creek have water in it?" he asked.

"It might have some flow during the wet season in July and August," Ducharme said. "But these washes are primarily formed by flash floods. You can have a thunderstorm anywhere in the watershed and it will turn this thing into a raging torrent in a matter of minutes."

"Should we be having lunch here?" Dagic quipped.

"I think we're safe for the moment."

When lunch was over, Ducharme led the group downstream to look at San Francisco Rapid. A minefield of boulders, washed out from the side canyon, split the Rio Grande's flow into a dozen channels. The clearest one ran close to the near shore, beneath an overhanging cliff.

"Stay right as you go under that cliff," he said. "Do not let yourself be pulled into that wall."

He pointed out an island at the base of the rapid. "Janey and I will go first. We'll pull onto the island. I'll be waiting there with a throw rope in case anyone goes over."

They walked back to the boats, Janey complaining about butterflies. Ducharme was reassuring. In fact, he told her he wanted her to pick the route. "You can see the rocks better than I can. If we're on a collision course, pick a direction and call it out. I'll go whichever way you say."

"Oh, God."

They pushed off shore and lined themselves up at the center of the drop. As they approached the boulder field, Janey found her voice. "Head right!"

He followed her lead, prying the stern to keep it line with the bow.

"Right again!" she called. "Now, straight!"

They cleared the last of the boulders and raced under the overhanging cliff. The wall rushed past just out of reach. In time, the water slowed. They turned into an eddy.

Janey crowed. "I did it!"

Ducharme stepped into the shallows and unclipped his throw rope. "Keep the boat here in case we have to rescue someone."

He tapped the top of her helmet and marched to the

head of the island.

Richard and Lara came next, deftly maneuvering through the boulders and the narrow channel. Lara beamed as she pulled up next to Janey. "What do you think of that, Mom?"

"Awesome!" she said.

Ducharme waved Archie and Parker on. They, too, executed picture perfect moves and came through without a scratch.

Dagic and Peter came last. They took a good line at the start, but near the bottom of the rapid, Peter inexplicably drew the bow crossways to the final boulder. Dagic backpaddled frantically, but it was too late. They hit the rock amidships and capsized, the boat pinning against the rock.

Peter washed through first, floating on his back with his feet in front. Ducharme tossed him the rope. Peter grabbed it and pulled himself to shore. He stood in the shallows, slipped and fell backwards on his ass. Dagic swam himself to shore. As he stepped out of the river, he glared at Peter.

"Don't you know left from right?"

"I'm sorry," Peter said. "I got confused."

"Jesus Christ!"

Ducharme intervened. "Alright, Janko, we've got a pinned canoe up there. Let's see what we can do."

He and Dagic walked to the head of the island and surveyed the situation. The canoe was in the middle of the river, wrapped like a horseshoe around the rock. The pinned canoe acted like a giant boulder, creating a short stretch of slow water amidst the raging current.

"We're going to have to ferry out and see if we can get

into that slow water," Ducharme said. "Do you know how to ferry, Janko?"

Dagic shook his head. Ducharme explained that by aiming a canoe upstream at a slight angle, it's possible to paddle across a strong current without losing ground.

"If we can get into that slow water behind the rock, we'll paddle up to the canoe and tie a rope to it. I've got a 75-footer in my boat."

He walked back to where the others stood waiting with anxious faces.

"We're going to try to pull the canoe off with a rope," he said. "I'm going to need all of you to help."

He and Dagic emptied the equipment out of his canoe and carried it up to the head of the island. Peter brought the box with the rope and assorted pulleys. Ducharme dropped the coiled rope in the canoe and settled into the stern.

"Are you ready, Janko?"

"Yes, sir."

With the boat aimed upstream, they paddled into the current, gradually making their way across the river. When they were directly downstream of the pinned canoe, he gave the order.

"Paddle hard!"

Dagic leaned forward and dug his paddle in, sending the boat surging forward. Ducharme had never felt anyone with his strength. In a matter of seconds, they had reached the pinned canoe. Dagic tied the rope to the handle and waved his hand.

"Go!" he said.

They let their canoe drift backwards, then angled towards the shore, the rope uncoiling as they went.

"Nice work, Janko," Peter said as they hit the bank.

There was fifteen feet of rope left. Ducharme ordered everyone to grab hold and dig their feet into the gravel bar. "This is a game of tug-of-war, but with real consequences," he said.

He took the last position, just behind Dagic. "Ready? One, two, three, pull!"

He leaned back and pulled with all his strength. The rope went taught. Grunts filled the air. The canoe didn't budge.

They leaned over to catch their breath. "One more time. One, two, three, pull!"

Nothing. They lowered the rope.

"Why don't we just leave it?" Lara said. "We're almost at the end of the trip."

Ducharme snapped. "That canoe costs more than a thousand dollars," he said. "I'm not going to leave it unless I absolutely have to."

Lara frowned. Janey put her arm around her. He felt bad about being short, but he was tired and anxious.

"We're going to have to try a Z-drag," he said. "Someone bring me that box with the rope and pulleys."

"You've got the equipment for a Z-drag?" Richard said.

"Every good river guide does. We pinned quite a few rafts on the Chattooga and that was the only way to get them off."

A Z-drag, he explained, was an arrangement of ropes and pulleys that effectively tripled the force of people pulling on a rope. The key was finding a tree or boulder within reach of the rope to which you could attach a pulley. There were no trees on the island, but Ducharme found a boulder the size of a garbage can. He tied a short piece of rope around it and clipped on a pulley. He ran the long rope through the pulley, tied another short loop to the long rope and attached a second pulley. Pulled tight, the long rope coming out from the canoe and through the two pulleys formed an elongated Z.

"O.K., folks, this is our last chance," he said. "Everybody grab on."

Again, he counted to three and gave the command to pull. This time, the canoe inched forward. They caught their breath and pulled a second time. Another three feet of canoe emerged. On the third try, the boat came free. Everyone cheered, but as they hauled the canoe to shore, the cheering stopped. The wooden center thwart was broken in half, the gunwales cracked. As the canoe touched shore, it rolled over like a dead whale.

"It's ruined, isn't it," Dagic said.

"It's pretty bad," Ducharme said. "The question is, can we get it in decent enough shape to paddle to the take out."

"How far is that?"

"About seventeen miles."

Peter came up. "I'm really sorry," he said. "This was my fault."

Ducharme began coiling the rope. "You and Janko get your gear out. We'll see what we can do about the hull."

When the gear was removed, he yanked off the splintered halves of the center thwart and threw them in the grass. People sensed his anger, kept their distance.

He turned to Janko. "Let's get this on flat ground. I'm going to try to stomp down the hull."

Set upright, the canoe looked like a red banana. Ducharme stepped in the middle and pushed down on the ends. The hull yielded briefly to his weight, but bent upward again when he stepped back.

"We need to sit this in the sun for awhile. The polyvinyl gets much more flexible when it heats up. Janko, let's put some big rocks in this thing. The rest of you see what of Janko and Peter's stuff you can fit in your boats. I'll make lunch in a little while."

He and Janko collected some heavy rocks and set them in the bow and stern so the hull sat straight. In his head, he added up his reduced profit from the probable loss of the canoe. He wasn't even sure he could get a new one in time for his next trip. That could be a disaster.

"Alright, let's leave this for about an hour."

He went to his canoe and pulled out the container with the lunch fixings.

"Let me help you," Parker said.

"Yes, we'll do it," Janey added. "Come on, Lara."

The women laid out the bread, meats and cheeses. People silently made their sandwiches and squatted on the rocky ground. The sun traveled in a slow arc across the sky.

Ducharme pulled his hat over his head, attempted to nap. He checked his watch. Napped some more.

"O.K., let's see if this thing will float," he said.

Peter and Janko jumped to their feet and helped him take the rocks out of the canoe. Despite a large wrinkle in the middle, the hull stayed reasonably flat. They carried the boat to the river. Peter and Janko sat in the seats.

"A bit wobbly," Janko said, "but I think we can make it."

He breathed a sigh of relief. "Alright, folks, we've got about five miles to the campsite. Pack up the lunch stuff and let's go."

Bone Watering Campground formed a large grassy bench on the Texas side of the river. Ranchers sometimes watered their cattle here, the trail they followed snaking down from a bluff through the prickly pear.

"This is a good part of the river to bathe," he said. "The current is slow and the bottom sandy. Let's make the area upstream of the campsite for the women and downstream for the men."

While the others set up their tents, he unrolled his sleeping bag in the grass and collapsed on top of it. He closed his eyes, felt the stress of the afternoon flow from his body into the beyond. That was a close call with the canoe. He could easily have lost the boat. Someone might have gotten hurt. Maybe he was asking too much taking people down the Lower Canyons. What choices did that leave him?

He awoke to the playful conversation of the women as they moved past him on their way to bathe. He sat up, slid off his shorts and wrapped a towel around his waist. The men were already in the water, laughing as they threw a bar of soap back and forth. It was a beautiful scene really, all these bodies in the warm Rio Grande. The evening sun gilded the top of the bluffs, horsetails streaming out across the sky. Rain tonight. Home tomorrow. He hung his towel on a bush and waded into the river.

|Twenty-Three|

Two weeks after arriving in Mexico City, Sayda and Kelin had arranged with a smuggler to drive them to Ciudad Acuna across the Rio Bravo from Del Rio, Texas. From the moment the driver dropped them off at the Parque Braulio overlooking the river, Sayda's spirits soared. Boys played soccer, children waded in the sapphire blue water. At the west end of the park, cars, trucks, and pedestrians crossed the Del Rio-Ciudad Acuna International Bridge into the United States. The United States!

But the bridge was for people with documentation. For her and Kelin, there was the river, and on the other side of the river was the wall. Slatted steel, 35 feet tall, it was impossible to climb without a very big ladder.

The safe house where Sayda and Kelin had been directed by the smuggler was disgusting—dirty, hot, devoid of furniture. She and Kelin slept on mats on the floor, four people to a room. Cockroaches darted around the edges, looking for crumbs of food. The toilet was so foul she and Kelin preferred to urinate in the backyard.

On the third day, the coyote appeared. He was not a fearsome looking man as she expected, just a mustachioed 30-something with a baseball cap and a white T-shirt. He shook hands with the eight people in the house who would be making the crossing. He would bring an extension ladder, which they would float across the river on an inner tube and lean up against the wall. They would lower themselves down the other side by a rope.

"The ladder does not reach the top of the wall, so you have to be able to pull yourself up another 3 or 4 feet." He nodded at Kelin. "You, with the missing hand, you will not be able to do that."

Sayda jumped in. "I'll go first and pull him up."

"It's up to you," the coyote said. "I take my payment up front. If he can't get over the wall, it's his problem."

The payment was $1,000 each, a third of it to go to the local drug mafia for "permission" to pass. Sayda contacted her mother, who wired the money to her. "We don't have much money left," her mother said. "You're going to have to make it."

At 10 pm, the coyote returned, transporting the immigrants in a windowless van to the outskirts of the city. The driver stopped, and after helping the coyote lower the extension ladder from the roof, sped off into the night. Sayda, Kelin and the six others—all men—followed the coyote down to the river. The sandy banks were mushy, their feet sinking up to the ankles. After setting down the ladder, the coyote fetched two inner tubes from the brush.

"You can hold onto one of these," he said to Kelin. "The others will have to swim."

The coyote laid the ladder across one of the inner tubes and set off swimming across the river. Sayda and Kelin followed, she pulling the tube from the front and Kelin kicking behind. In minutes, they were across the river and slogging through the mush on the other side.

The wall looked much higher than it did at a distance. The coyote moved along its base until he found a solid piece of ground, then he and another man leaned the ladder up against it.

"When you get to the top," he told the man, "tie the rope to the top rung and toss it over the wall. Don't start lowering yourself down until another man is on the ladder."

The man started up the ladder with the rope coiled over his shoulder. He reached the top, tossed the rope over the side, and called down. "Venga!"

Sayda waited nervously as the coyote directed the next man up the ladder. The third went up and over and then the fourth. When the sixth man reached the top, he hesitated. There was a commotion on the other side of the wall. A light flashed upward. The man ducked. "Policia!" he hissed.

"Bajar!" the coyote yelled.

Sayda pleaded. "Let us go up. We don't care if we're caught."

The coyote shook his head. "No. We're on American soil. If they catch me, they'll put me in jail. And they'll send you and your brother back."

Carrying the ladder, they scrambled down the bank and back across the river.

***

In the coming days, Sayda fell into despair. She found herself thinking of what she and Kelin had left behind—their friends, now back at school, their mother, alone and suffering. And the land—the green hills, the narrow streets where they'd played as children. If everything worked out as planned, they would never see home again. What kind of a dream was that?

The coyote reappeared. He had another plan for the four who didn't make it over the wall.

"It's become too difficult to cross here," he said. "You need to go west, into the canyon country where the wall ends. I have a friend who will drive you most of the way, but you have to be prepared to walk through the desert—at least 30 miles to the river and 30 more after that. My friend will only charge you $500 each, but he will not go with you to the river. You will be on your own."

The two men exchanged glances. "Sesente millas. Esta muy lejos."

"Can you wade across the river?" Kelin asked. "I have only one hand."

"You can wade," the coyote said. "It's very shallow. And there will be no border patrol. No cameras. It's wilderness."

Sayda and Kelin exchanged glances. "We can do it," she said.

She spoke to her mother that night. "I can send you $1,000, but that's the end of the money," she said. "I've sold everything except the house."

Over the following day, she and Kelin ate everything

they could get their hands on. They ditched their extra clothes and stuffed their backpacks with tortillas wrapped in foil and water bottles scrounged from garbage cans.

When the new coyote arrived in the morning, he was driving not a van but a small, beat up sedan. The tires were bald, the windows caked with dirt. Sayda squeezed in the back seat between Kelin and one of the men with a scar across his cheek. The other man sat up front.

"We drive for four hours," the coyote said. "All dirt road."

The last tree she saw was in a gulley a few miles out of town, the last house a few miles beyond that. The landscape held nothing for the eye but an endless sea of low bluffs transected by arroyos devoid of water. The tires grumbled over the dirt road, popping when they spat out a rock. The hot desert air blasted through the open windows.

Rendered drowsy by the mid-day heat, Sayda fell asleep. At one point she awoke to find the man with the scar looking down her blouse. Instead of turning away, he just grinned.

The car slowed. Were they here already? The car came to a halt, the engine ticking in the heat.

"Flat tire," the driver said.

Sayda felt suddenly claustrophobic. "Let me out," she said to Kelin.

The heat hit her like a door being opened on an oven. She shielded her eyes from the sun, stared at the horizon. There were no signs of civilization, not even a fence line. Cholla cactus reached their spindly arms to the empty sky. A cindercone rose to the west, umber rocks spilling down its steep slopes. This was a frightening land.

While the driver fetched the spare out of the trunk, she walked into a gulley to take a pee. They would not last long out here if the car broke down. She would never venture more than a mile or so into this country on her own, and now they were facing a walk of thirty miles just to the river.

The driver called them and they headed back on the road.

"How much longer?" the man up front said.

"Two hours," the driver said.

"Two hours? Shit, man. We've already been driving for three. Where exactly are you taking us?"

"To the arroyo. The arroyo will take you to the river."

"Why don't you just drive us to the river from here?"

"There's no access."

"What do you mean? I've seen tracks heading in that direction."

"Those go to private ranches," the driver said. "They don't go to the river." The driver glared. "You want to walk? I'll let you out now and you can walk. The buzzards will be picking your bones before you ever see the river."

Sayda began to worry. Was this all a set-up? Take the immigrants' money and dump them in the desert? It would be easy to do.

Finally, the car descended a slope and slowed to a halt. The driver stepped out, pointed to an arroyo twisting away to the north. "This is it."

"How do you know this is the right one?" the man with the scar said. "It looks just like all the others we've seen."

"Trust me," the driver said. "You see those footprints? I have taken others here before. Just last week."

Kelin and Sayda exchanged glances.

"How long will it take is to get to the river?" she asked.

The driver shrugged. "Two, maybe three days. Less if you walk through the night."

"Where do we go after we cross the river?" Kelin said.

"There's a dirt road on the other side. You'll see it. It's about twenty miles to Sanderson. You can hitch a ride north from there."

The man with the scar spoke to her. "You won't need to hitchhike. We have a friend in Fort Stockton. As soon as we call him, he'll come pick us up."

The driver asked if there was anything else they needed. Yes, they had their water bottles and a little bit of food. They had their cell phones, though they wouldn't work out here.

The driver waved. "Adios, amigos. Buena suerte."

|Twenty-Four|

The last night's dinner was an upbeat affair, which Ducharme finished off with a dessert of stewed apples topped with Red Hots and chopped pecans. Richard built a fire of mesquite and salt cedar scrounged from the riverside. People reminisced about their favorite parts of the trip, capsizes and near misses. Janey seemed in a joyful mood, laughing about how she and Lara ran into the reeds.

With the dishes cleaned and the group gathered around the fire, Archie proposed a topic of conversation— talk about the biggest mistake you've made in your life and what you learned from it. Participation wasn't mandatory, but if you weren't going to talk, you had to go elsewhere.

Dagic scowled. "Why do you want to spoil everything by having people talk about their mistakes?"

"Because it's a great way for everybody to learn something," Archie said. "Most of us are at stage in life where we don't have to pretend. We can be honest about who we really are."

Dagic shook his head. "You Americans think that by talking about everything, you can make the pain go away. Is bullshit."

He got up and walked away.

Ducharme was not surprised. More than ever, he

thought this man was hiding something. Something big.

"Mom, are you going to talk about Dad?" Lara said.

"I might. Yes."

"Oh, God." She, too, got up and left.

Archie looked around the group. "Alright, who wants to go first?" he said.

"Why don't you?" Peter said. "You're the one who proposed it."

Archie proceeded to talk about the time he read his eldest daughter's diary when she was a senior in high school. "I don 't know why I went into her room," he said in all seriousness. "Well, I guess I do know why. I thought there might be something going on with this African-American boy. I found her diary in the top drawer of her dresser and went straight to the end. She talked about being in love with him. An African-American! I was really upset. I didn't really know this guy. I heard he was a nice kid, but I just couldn't stand the thought of Emily having a serious relationship with a black man. I told Gail about it. She was furious that I had gone into Emily's diary, but she was more concerned about this relationship.

"When Emily came home, we sat her down and talked to her," Archie said. "I told her I was the one who had read her diary. She went crazy. I knew right away I'd made a mistake. She couldn't believe I'd violated her privacy like that. I don't think she ever forgave me until she went off to college, and even then things were never quite the same."

Archie took off his glasses and wiped away a tear. He went on to say that what he'd learned is, no matter how much you think you owe it to your children to steer them away from the perils of life, you should never violate their trust. "Once that's gone, you have no hope of convincing them of anything," he said.

Ducharme was stunned by the honesty of Archie's story, and by his depth of emotion in telling it. He'd taken Archie for a frivolous character, but now saw him in a totally different light. He wished Dagic had been there to hear it.

Peter volunteered next. "Some people might say my biggest mistake was today, pulling right instead of left," he said.

Everyone laughed.

"It'd be good to get that down before the end of the trip, Pooh Bear," Ducharme said.

Pooh Bear went on to say his biggest mistake was getting married when he knew that he was gay.

"I had never come out to anyone at the time. I was raised a Baptist and was living in a small town, so that kind of thing was not tolerated. My mother would have been crushed and my father probably would have killed me. So I went ahead with the marriage just hoping things would work out. They did for awhile, then Anne began to suspect there was something wrong. I finally admitted it to her. She was shocked and disgusted. She ended up filing for divorce about a week later."

"At least you didn't have children," Janey said.

"Yeah, but I wasted years of my life. And Anne's, too. And I hated myself for being a phony."

Again, he wished Dagic was here. He would learn how this man had suffered, how the last thing he needed was to be berated in public.

Then Parker spoke up. She told an improbable story of having been in beauty pageants as a young girl.

"I didn't have a big old butt like I do now," she said.

She talked about being totally under the control of her mother and a coach, who told her what to eat and what not to eat.

"I had to send pictures of what I was eating to my coach!" she said, eliciting groans of disbelief from the group.

"This went on for years. When I finally graduated from pageants, I didn't know how or what to eat. I had no voice of my own. I became really depressed. It took me years to get over it. All I can say is, don't ever do that to a child."

Richard came next. He confessed that his story was nowhere near as dramatic as the others. "My mistake is that I'd always wanted to be a history teacher," he said. "I love history, can't read enough books. But I didn't have the guts to go the academic route. I worried I wouldn't make enough money as a high school teacher and didn't want to invest the time and money to go to graduate school. So, I became a realtor."

"You've still got time," Parker said. "You could teach at a community college."

"Maybe, once I retire," Richard said. "Still, I feel like I made a mistake not going after it the first time."

Now, it was down to Ducharme and Janey. He knew what his big mistake was, but didn't know if he could or should confess it. Janey spared him for a time.

"As you know, I'm separated from my husband, and I expect our divorce to come through shortly after I return," she said. "I could say marrying Worth was a mistake, but I couldn't have known that at the time. He seemed like such a lovely person to me. And we've two wonderful children, which I wouldn't change for the world. I can't tell you how desperately I needed to be loved by someone and how good it felt at the time. So I went and had an affair, and I've been paying for it ever since."

Janey held her face in her hands. Parker, sitting next to her, gave her a hug.

"I was so ashamed when it came to light," she said. "The girls couldn't look at me. Worth was furious, though he hadn't loved me for years. He saw the affair totally as a way to get back at me, and he's been punishing me for it ever since. He's told all our friends that that's the reason the marriage is breaking up. He's used it with lawyers as a way to get more money. I know I haven't heard the end of it."

She blew her nose in a handkerchief. "Anyway, I've learned that having even a brief affair is a terrible idea when you're still in a relationship."

Heads nodded all around. One by one, they fixed on him. He had two major mistakes he could confess. He chose the lesser.

"I have a lady friend back in Aintry," he said. "She's a vet by the name of Carmen. She's a beautiful person, and I really fell for her. But she was hesitant to commit because she doubted I could make this business work. She thought if it failed that I would move back East. I assured her I'd make the business work. Then, I made a really big-ass mistake."

He went on to describe how he left the door to the operating room ajar, and the dog, Precious, racing out and getting run over by the truck.

"She's really never forgiven me for that. I can't blame her."

Voices exhaled around the circle. Parker touched his

arm. "She may forgive you yet."

"As for what I've learned, I'd like to say pay attention to the little things, because they can have big consequences. But do you live your life thinking if you don't close every door, if you fool around for just a minute, someone or something could get killed? I don't know. That's a hard way to live."

Murmurs rose and fell like the sparks from the fire. A bottle of bourbon was passed around. He waved it off.

"I'd love to stay up with you all, but after today's adventure, I'm beat."

"No shit," Richard said.

"Tomorrow, we should reach the takeout about noon. Hopefully, the shuttle driver will be there with the van. We'll pack up and head back to Midland-Odessa. It's been a great trip. I can't thank you guys enough."

"You da man!" Archie said.

He left the campfire and walked by starlight down to his canoe. He unrolled his sleeping bag, brushed his teeth, and spat into the river. Glancing upstream, he saw Dagic crouching by the shore. He walked over and stood beside him.

"Nice night," he said.

Dagic glanced at him. "Feeling better, are we?"

He swallowed the dig. "You know, people told some amazing stories tonight. You might feel differently about certain of our tripmates if you'd heard them."

"I heard them."

"Oh, so, you broke the rules. You were supposed to tell your story if you listened to the others."

"I don't think anyone wants to hear my story. It doesn't have a happy ending."

He knelt down, flipped a pebble into the river. "Let's hear it."

Dagic stared up at the stars. "There are some sins that cannot be forgiven. God's punishment is to force you to play them over and over in your mind. That's my story."

He pursed his lips. "Yeah, I know something about that."

"Really? A dead dog?"

"No. Something else." His thoughts went back to the Chattooga. To a yellow raft colliding with a rock, kids falling in the water. But he was not going to go there. Not tonight.

"Well, I'm going to hit the rack," he said.

Dagic mock saluted. "Sweet dreams."

|Twenty-Five|

Gallagher was brought naked into the Presidio Police Department, where he was issued a blue jump suit and a pair of plastic flip flops. He was charged with exposing himself to a minor and put in a cell with a twenty-year-old white kid.

"Nice to see a brother," Gallagher said, as the jailer closed the door behind him. "Danny Gallagher. They call me El Chompo."

The kid sat up on his bed and wiped his hand across his close-cropped hair. "Wells Fargo."

Gallagher stared. "That some kind of joke?"

"No, sir. That's what my parents named me."

He shook his head. "So, Wells Fargo, what are you in for?"

"Auto theft. 'Cept I didn't really steal it. More like borrowed it."

"They charged me with exposing myself to a minor. I was just trying to borrow some clothes."

"What happened to your clothes?"

"Some Mexicans jumped me and stripped me naked."

"Shit. Why'd they do that?"

"Just mean, I guess."

"Fuckin' wets."

He sat on his bunk, tested the springs. "I'm going to see the magistrate tomorrow and get this straightened out. I don't plan to spend more than one night in this shithole."

"I hear that."

He laid back in his cot and stared at the ceiling. "I need to find someplace to stay. I got me an Airstream I had parked down at the Hoodoos campground, but I've kind of worn out my welcome there. You know of any place along the river where I won't be charged? I like being down by the river."

Wells thought. "If you go out U.S. 90 just past Sanderson, there's a gravel road to the right called Bone Water. That'll take you all the way down to the river. It's a long twenty miles, but it's real nice down there. No one'll bother you."

"Bone Water. I'll have to check it out."

The following morning, Officer Menendez brought Gallagher before the magistrate, who read out the charge.

"Exposing yourself to a minor. Is that right, Mr. Gallagher?"

"Your honor, that's not how it went down," he said. "Mexicans robbed my clothes and locked me out of my trailer. I was just knocking on doors trying to borrow a pair of Levis."

The judge looked over his glasses. "Officer Menendez, do you consider this man a danger to the community?"

"Yes, I do, your honor. Two nights ago, he ran over a UDI with an ATV. We didn't charge him for that."

The judge scribbled on a piece of paper. "Mr. Gallagher, you are instructed to appear in court next Wednesday at 9 am. Bond is set at $3,000."

"Sir, I don't have that kind of money."

"Talk to a bondsman. There's a couple of cards on the wall."

Gallagher stared at the cards, jotted down the first one that grabbed his eye—Tito Craig at A-1 Bonds. He called the number and explained his situation. Craig asked if he had anything that could be used in lieu of cash.

"I've got an Airstream trailer worth at least $3,000."

"Do you have a title for that?"

"Yes, sir. It's in the trailer. We'll need a locksmith to get inside."

Freed from the Presidio jail, Gallagher drove to the Hoodoos Campground where he met the bondsman and the locksmith. Craig took a quick look inside the trailer and pronounced his satisfaction.

"I'll see you Wednesday at 9," he said. "You try runnin,' it won't take long to find you."

"Wouldn't think of it," Gallagher said.

He packed his clothes, binoculars and pistol into his duffel, kissed his trailer goodbye, and headed east along the River Road, whooping like a kid as he flew over the dips and rises.

In Terlingua, he stopped at the Cottonwood General Store and bought three day's worth of Wolf Brand Chili, Slim Jims, and Bruce's Pecan Pies. On to Shot Time Liquor, he bought a six-pack of Pabst Blue Ribbon beer and a bottle of El Jimador.

Heading north through the Chihuahuan Desert, he opened the tequila and threw down a long mouthful. As the liquor warmed his throat, he started to sing. "*Hey, Joe, where you going with that gun in your hand? I said, hey, Joe, where you going with that gun in your hand?*"

Out on the horizon, the shed-roofed silhouette of the

U.S. Border Patrol station appeared.

"Oh, shit."

He fumbled for the top of the bottle, couldn't find it. He slowed down, pulled to the shoulder of the road. Unable to find the cap, he cranked down the window and threw the bottle into the brush. He pulled back onto the road and slowed to a halt in the shadow of the roof. An armed guard approached the driver's side, while another with a German Shepherd waited in the wings.

"Afternoon, sir. Are you a U.S. citizen?"

"Yes, sir. Texas born and raised."

"Can I see some I.D.?"

He reached for his wallet, handed him his driver's license.

"You mind telling me why you pulled over back there?"

"I was looking for my wallet. I had it stashed in my duffel."

The guard studied his driver's license. "Where are you headed, Mr. Gallagher?"

He hesitated. "Nowhere in particular," he said.

"Nowhere in particular?"

"I'm thinking of camping out down by the river."

"The river's the other way."

"Down past Sanderson. I don't like the crowds in the park."

The guard motioned to his partner to bring on the dog.

"Do you mind stepping out of the vehicle, sir?"

"Not at all, not at all."

As soon as his feet hit the ground, Gallagher's head began to spin. It was all he could do to keep from toppling over. He watched the dog as it nosed its way around the truck. Surely, it smelled the booze, but that was not what it was trained to alert on. That would be drugs and humans.

"I'll bet that dog can smell a Mexican a mile away," he said.

"They don't discriminate by nationality," the guard said.

"I got robbed by a bunch of 'em last week down at the Hoodoos Campground."

"That was you? I heard about that."

"That was me."

"I guess you got your clothes back."

"This is what I had in my trailer."

The guard with the dog nodded to his partner. The latter returned his wallet.

"You're free to go. Try to stay out of trouble."

He snapped to attention and saluted. "Yes, sir. Thank you, sir."

Back on the highway, he breathed a sigh of relief. He could really use that drink now. God damn! He grew depressed at the thought of having to throw a half-full bottle away. That was supposed to last him through the afternoon.

He reached the town of Aintry, its dusty sidewalk empty of people, its paltry storefronts dark. Where was a bar when you needed one? East of town, the two-lane highway ran straight and flat through a featureless plain. No mesas to draw the eye, no bends to command your attention. Out on the chalk white ground, a lone cow stared at nothing. That was old Danny, a sorry-ass cowboy with no money, no friends, and no purpose for living other than to shove food down his gullet. He was a desperado in the true meaning of the word—a man without hope.

East of Sanderson, he found an unmarked and almost unrecognizable road heading to the south. He hoped this was Bone Water Road, but he wouldn't bet his last dime on it. He crossed the cattle grate and headed into the desert, not a house or a phone pole in sight. Gravel popped beneath his tires. He checked his gas gauge—half a tank. If he became stranded out here, he might not be found for a week. The land around him was like a vast, frozen ocean— wave after wave of hard packed soil speckled with creosote bush. He began to suspect that Mr. Wells Fargo was mistaken, or more likely a liar.

Then came a crack in the horizon, a line of rimrock. The road circled and ended at the top of a bluff. He parked the truck and walked to the edge. Three hundred feet below him, the Rio Grande stretched away to the north and south. Four canoes were pulled on the near shore and four tents pitched in the grass. Standing in the water, their backs to him, were three naked women.

He hurried to his truck, got his binoculars out of his duffel bag, and lay down at the edge of the bluff. There were some men bathing downstream, but they were of no interest to him. He focused in on the first woman. She was heavy set, folds of skin marking her back and saggy bottom. Not much to look at there. The next woman was slimmer, had a nice ass. He could only see a fraction of her tits, but they looked tantalizing, too. The third one looked younger than the others, maybe one of them's daughter. She had a really sweet ass, firm as an apple. She dove into the water and started breaststroking upstream, the water swirling each time she snapped her long legs together.

Her heard a whoop and panned back to the woman in

the middle. She had ducked underwater and come back up facing him. Her titties were in plain view, her bush just above the waterline. She began soaping her underarms and then her breasts. Goddamn, what a show! He watched her for awhile, then panned back to the girl. She had rolled onto her back. What was this? A shiny taco!

He unzipped his fly, drew out his cock, and started to masturbate. Never before had he done this at a live show, and this one was a triple header. He panned back to the woman in the middle. She was looking downstream, checking on the men. That could only mean she was about to go for the gold. Sure enough, she reached down and started soaping her bush. She rubbed it nice and slow, building a mound of suds. Gallagher whipped himself to a peak, let out a groan, and shot semen all over the rocks.

After a time, he got up and went to the truck for some tissue. He wiped off his cock and tucked it back in his trousers. He got a beer out of the cooler and a package of Slim Jims and went back to his lookout. The women had come out of the water and were toweling themselves dry. He turned to study the men. Which one of those bastards was the guide? If it was the one who duked him out in Terlingua, he might try to find a way to retaliate. Toss a few rocks at him while he was paddling down the river. There was one tall dude, too old for a guide. Same with two of the others. But one fit the mold—young, buff, and tanned.

He downed his beer and ate a few Slim Jims. The young guy dressed and went over to a canoe with a stove set on top. Definitely the guide. The big guy came over, exchanged a few words with him. They both looked up at the bluff. Gallagher ducked back. If they'd seen him, they'd put two and two together and realize he'd been spying on the women. He slipped back to the truck, got out his pistol, and stood watching the trail.

After downing two more beers, he decided no one was coming. He went back to the edge. The big dude was walking along the shore carrying an armful of driftwood. He dropped it by a fire pan and went looking for more. The others came out of their tents and stood around the guide while he cooked. Time for his own dinner.

He went to the truck, opened a can of chili and sat sideways in the passenger seat with the door open. Off to the west, a solid bank of clouds stretched out from the horizon. Might come a rain later tonight, but in the mean time, it was putting on a fine light show. As the sun dropped behind the clouds, it lit up the edges pussy pink. How lucky was he to witness this, to see all this country spread before him?

As darkness came on, the campers lit a fire and sat around in a circle. He picked up his binoculars and studied their faces. Only one person seemed to be talking, the others looking on intently. Must be story time.

After awhile, all eyes settled on the guide, whose back was to him. The middle-aged woman who'd tantalized him in the river was staring intently, her face in the firelight a thing of beauty. Mr. Big must have a riveting tale to tell.

Truth be told, he'd give anything to be in on their conversation. Many was the time he'd captivated his cowboy pals around a campfire or a bar, spilling tales of daring-do or humor. How he missed those days.

A heaviness settled in his heart and he wondered how much of his present situation was his own fault and how much the fickle hand of fate? He'd made some mistakes here and there. He'd driven off his wife with his drinking and a lot of his friends sided with her after the divorce. Then, he got fired from the ranch, which hurt more than he cared to admit. There was this mess with the Border Brigade. And now the trailer park fiasco. Old Danny wasn't a quitter, but it was getting late in the game and he wasn't holding many cards. He needed some kind of miracle, or he just might fold 'em right here.

|Twenty-Six|

By the time Janey got back to the tent, Lara was asleep. She took off her bra, stripped down to her panties, and put on her nightshirt. It was too hot to get in her sleeping bag, so she lay on top staring into the near darkness. She couldn't shake the image of Robbie in the firelight, his haunted eyes and hollow voice. Had she really said to him that he hadn't known hard times? She rolled over and tried to sleep. Not happening.

Lara's steady breathing confirmed that her daughter was, in fact, asleep. As quietly as possible, she slipped on a pair of socks, unzipped the tent, and stepped out into the night. Stars illuminated the dark imprint of the trail through the grass. She followed it to the kitchen and down to the river.

Robbie lay sleeping by the water's edge. She knelt down, touched his shoulder. His eyes snapped open.

"Do you need something?" he said.

She put her forefinger in front of her lips. "Couldn't sleep."

He propped himself up on his elbows. "You, too?"

She nodded. "I am so sorry for what happened to you. Maybe things will work out with this vet."

"I doubt it, but thanks for the thought. I'm sorry for

your trouble, too."

She leaned forward and kissed him on the mouth.

He waited for her to pull back. "Was that sympathy, or what?" he said.

"That was affection for an honest man."

"I'd say half-honest."

"What do you mean?"

He took a deep breath. "Leaving Carmen's door open wasn't my biggest mistake. I did something much worse."

He went on to recount the day on the Chattooga, his raft filled with young women, the approach to the rapid known as Jawbone. "Our procedure was to never head into Jawbone without getting the go-ahead from one of the kayakers," he said. "The reason was, if one raft tipped over, the guys on shore would have time to get everybody out of the water before the next raft came through. I just assumed that Temo had made it. He always did. But when I came around the bend, his raft was upside down and his passengers were all over the place. I managed to avoid them by paddling hard toward mid-river, but that put me in the path of this rock called Hydro. We hit that sucker and my kids started falling out. It was a real shit show."

He looked off into the dark.

"This one little girl, Maria, got swept into this bad-ass rapid called Soc 'Em Dog. It's got a hydraulic at the bottom, one of these reverse waves that won't let you go. I paddled across the river, but by the time I got to her, it was too late. She was being rolled over and over. All I could do was stand there and watch."

Janey exhaled. "Oh, my God. Did you get her out?"

"My friend, Temo, came over in a kayak. He was the strongest member of our team. He tried to paddle up to the rapid from below, but it was no use. Our lead guide, Annie, came over. She said she would take the others down and call the Rescue Squad, but we knew that would take hours. After she left, Temo got this idea of floating a log into the rapid and knocking her out. We went up in the woods and found one, rolled it down to the shore. That thing went over the drop and pushed her right out. She was completely blue by then. I keep seeing her face, her eyes wide open..."

She put her hand to his face, felt the stubble on his cheeks. "So that's why you left."

"I got fired. I thought it was unfair. I convinced myself that the accident wasn't my fault. But it was."

He shook his head. "I couldn't stick around the Southeast. No one would hire me. So, I came out West to make a new start. I haven't told anybody about this, because I was afraid it would get around that I was not to be trusted."

"You haven't told anybody? Not even Carmen?"

"You're the first." His eyes filled with tears. "I keep seeing her over in my mind. Her face turned blue. I've got to get that out of my head."

"You know you can trust me. I won't tell anyone you don't want me to tell."

Their mouths fell open, her tongue reaching to find his. He had one golden rule—never get romantically involved with a client on a trip. He was going to break it.

"Let's go for a paddle," he said. "We'll take the busted canoe. No center thwart to get in the way."

She helped him lift the canoe into the river and spread the sleeping bag on the wrinkled floor. He tiptoed into the water and held the canoe while she got in the front seat.

"You don't need a paddle," he said.

He steered the canoe into the middle of the river, to the wide, still pool where they had earlier bathed.

"Come sit between my legs," he said.

Holding onto the gunwales, she pushed herself off the seat and worked her way backwards. "Nice not to have that center thwart," she said.

He set his paddle aside and slipped down off the stern seat. She leaned back against his chest, her arms around his legs. The sky was littered with stars, framed by the canyon walls like the barrel of a telescope.

"Do you know your constellations?" she said.

"That's Orion. Follow his belt to Perseus. That's about all I know."

The boat drifted into a midstream eddy and began a slow spin. It seemed like the sky was turning, not the canoe. She lost all sense of bearing, felt adrift in space.

A hand reached down and unbuttoned her shirt, bared her breasts to the sky. Fingers traced slow circles around her nipples, sending an electric current into her thighs. After years of being dammed, the river within her began to flow.

"Are you sure this is O.K.?" she said.

"Yes."

"Can we do it without tipping over?"

"If we're careful. Bring your knees to your chest and slowly turn around."

She pivoted atop the sleeping bag, giggling as she completed the turn. He was smiling for the first time in days.

"Now, lay back."

The stars again came into view. She raised her hips

and he slid off her panties. One by one, he draped her legs over the sides of the canoe. She felt the cool night air against her thighs.

"You're never supposed to grab the gunwales," he said, "But I'm going to make an exception."

"Robbie, if you tip us over..."

He leaned forward, hands on the gunwales, and ever so carefully, entered her. She moaned, louder than she'd intended. He silenced her with a kiss. In the slowest and gentlest of motions, they made love beneath the spinning stars, afloat on the Rio Grande.

|Twenty-Seven|

Ducharme awoke to a scream. It was some distance away, upriver. A human scream, for sure. He sat up in his canoe. The moon was just disappearing behind a fast-moving wall of clouds. In the distance, a rumble of thunder. The landscape went dark, so dark he couldn't distinguish the canyon walls from the sky. He waited. A second clap of thunder, closer this time. He switched on his headlamp and stepped into the grass, searching for the duffel bag holding the last tent. A second headlamp appeared—Dagic.

"I was just about to look for you," Ducharme said. He found the duffel bag and pulled out the tent. "Let's get this thing up."

They unrolled the tent on the ground and started assembling the poles.

"Did you heard that scream?" Dagic said.

"I heard something."

"That was a man, Robbie."

"Could have been a mountain lion."

"I know it when I hear it. That was a man."

The rain hit just as they got the tent staked to the ground. Each ran back for his sleeping bag and clothes and ducked in the tent. It was tight quarters for the two men, their shoulders touching as they lay on their bags.

"We got that up just in time," Ducharme said.

"Yah. Just in time to finish your lovemaking."

He said nothing. He should have known that Dagic would be watching, listening.

"Sound travels in these canyons," Dagic said. "You can hear every confession, every moan..."

"Alright, asshole."

Dagic leaned toward him. "You broke the rules, Robbie."

A flash of lightning illuminated the tent, followed by a clap of thunder that echoed down the canyon like a series of cannon shots. Wind whipped through the campsite, the tent fabric straining against the poles. A hollow thud landed nearby. Ducharme sat up on his elbows.

"The canoes!"

He turned on his headlamp, unzipped the fly and stuck his head outside. The whole campsite seemed to be coming apart. Tarpaulins flapped in the wind. The canoe used as the kitchen counter had blown over and rolled across the ground.

"We need to load these boats with rocks or they'll end up in the river!"

He jumped out into the pouring rain, followed by Dagic. The men searched the ground for big rocks, carried them to the canoes and set them in the hulls. When the boats were weighed down to their satisfaction, they ran back to the tent.

Ducharme pulled his clothes off and hunted out a dry pair of underwear. "Thanks for the help," he said.

"No problem."

He shut off the headlamp and crawled into his sleeping bag. Dagic was silent, sulking. The man was hot for Janey, and she'd spurned him. The fucking guide got the prize. Now, even the gods were angry. If the rain kept up, the river might flood. He should wake everyone and tell them to move to higher ground. But it was late and he was tired. Too tired to fight any more.

By dawn, the rain had stopped. Ducharme emerged from the tent to find everything more or less intact. The canoes were all accounted for and the tarps still tied to the equipment. The river was high and muddy, swirling between the banks where last night it had been as still as a pond.

Richard came out of his tent. "What a storm last night!"

"Yeah, it nearly blew our canoes into the river," he said. "Janko and I had to weigh them down with rocks."

He asked Richard to help him turn the canoe upside down and stabilize it for cooking. He got the stove out and started the water boiling.

"The river looks high," Richard said. "Is that going to be a problem?"

"Shouldn't be. There's only one rapid, Sanderson Canyon, between here and the takeout. It's similar to San Francisco with lots of boulders in the channel, but I think it'll actually be easier with all this water."

He stole a glance at Janey's tent, eager to learn her mood after their midnight outing. He mixed up the hot chocolate and brewed the coffee.

"A Mocha Robbie for you, Richard?"

"Absolutely. I'm going to miss this."

Parker came out of her tent, followed by Archie and Lara. Finally, Janey emerged. She glanced at the river, then came into the kitchen and grabbed a cup. They exchanged smiles as he poured her coffee.

The conversation was all about the storm.

"Did you hear the thunder echoing down the canyon?" Parker said.

"Yeah, it sounded like a giant bowling ball bouncing between gutters," Archie said.

"I thought our tent was going to blow away."

He served up pancakes and bacon with instructions for everybody to eat as much as they wanted. "I don't plan to take any of this home with me."

When breakfast was over, he asked for help cleaning the dishes. Janey volunteered. They squatted together at the river's edge, conversing in low tones.

"Are you O.K. this morning?" he asked.

"Yes. And you?"

"I'm good."

He scrubbed the plates and handed them to her to rinse. As they neared the end of the dishes, he realized this might well be the last time he and Janey would speak in private. At the takeout, everyone would pile into the van for the long drive to the motel. They would say their goodbyes in the parking lot and he would drive back to Aintry alone.

Janey emptied out the dishwater and stood. His heart swelled with emotion.

"I don't want this to be the last time I see you," he said.

She stopped just behind him and touched a finger to the nape of his neck.

|Twenty-Eight|

The car disappeared over the bluff and the silence rushed in. Sayda felt frightened for her and Kelin to be alone with these two men, especially the one with the scar.

"Eh, muchacha, como se llama usted?" he said.

"I'm Sayda. This is my brother, Kelin."

"I'm Angel. This one is Jorge. You stick with us. We'll keep the mountain lions away."

She wondered if that was a real threat or if he was making this up. She had no knowledge of this barren country. It was nothing like the lush hills of home.

Angel checked his watch. "Five o'clock. It'll be dark in an hour. Let's get going."

She held Kelin back. "Let them go first."

They stepped into the arroyo and started walking. The sand was soft, her ankles bending left and right. She was thankful for the conditioning she'd gained from her years of soccer. Even so, thirty miles of this was going to be tough.

Angel turned to her again. "Where are you from, muchacha?"

She remained silent, not wanting to encourage this man to get close. Kelin answered. "San Pedro Sula."

"Us, too. Did the gangs chase you out?"

"They killed our father."

"Too bad. They killed Jorge's brother."

Angel pointed to Kelin's bandaged stump. "What happened there?"

"I fell off a train in Oaxaca."

Angel winced. "Sounds like you've had a hard trip."

"Yeah, it's been really bad."

Sayda felt a sudden urge to cry, but pushed it back down. She was not going to show any weakness to these men.

"You must be twins, eh? Two pretty faces."

She shot him a look.

Angel laughed. "Your sister doesn't talk much, eh, Kelin? I always say talk while you can. Soon enough, we'll be silent forever."

She pushed that thought away, too. Keep walking, she said to herself. Think only of the river.

The sun sank low, leaving the arroyo in shadow. She welcomed the relief from the heat, but so did the desert's creatures. Angel grabbed Jorge.

"Cuidado!"

They froze. Two steps in front of Jorge's open-toed sandal, a black scorpion stood on the sand, claws held open, stinger arched high over its back. Sensing no danger, it continued on across the arroyo.

"If he'd stung you, you'd be hurting, Jorge."

"We should walk slower," Jorge said.

"Walk any slower and we'll never get to the river. You need to keep your eyes open."

Evening gave way to twilight, the stars coming out in the cloudless sky. Jorge started lagging behind.

"When are we going to stop?" he moaned. "My knees

are killing me."

"We can stop here," Angel said. "But just for a water break."

They sat in the sand and dug out their water bottles. Sayda unwrapped a tortilla and split it with Kelin.

"What are your plans when you get across the river?" Angel said.

"We're going to apply for asylum," Kelin said.

"Because of your father?"

"Yes. The gangs threatened me, too."

"Do you have proof?"

"We have a newspaper article about our father's murder."

Angel pursed his lips. "Might work. Might not. They want proof that you're threatened because of your political views. You should come with me to a sanctuary city—San Antonio, Austin. At least the local cops won't bother you there."

"Sanctuary city, bullshit," Jorge said. "The Yankees hate us. I'm going to Canada."

Angel laughed. "You're going to Canada. You'll be lucky to make it across the river in those cheap sandals."

Jorge studied his smooth-soled, open-toed footwear. "They're Dona Michis," he said. "They're good."

"Sure, for walking down the street, not the desert."

Sayda tossed her wrapper in the sand and resumed walking. It was full dark now with no moon. The air grew chilly, the banks of the arroyo ever higher.

She didn't see the snake until just before she lowered her foot. She cried out, jumped to the side, knocking Kelin to the ground. The snake snapped into a coil, filled the air with a buzzing like a mariachi in hyperspeed.

"That's it," Angel said. "It's too dangerous to go on."

He gave the snake a wide berth, walked up to the west-facing wall and put his hand on it. "We should sleep here against this rock. It'll hold the sun's heat for awhile."

"But that's where the snakes are," Kelin said.

"If we sleep together, we'll be alright."

Kelin all but fell over in the sand, clutching his good arm to his chin.

"I am so tired," he said.

Sayda put her hand on his shoulder. "That's O.K. You're doing good."

"Come next to me, Sayda," Angel said. "You'll be warmer."

She shook her head. "I'm fine."

She lay down against her brother's back, whispered in his ear. "Stay next to me, O.K.?"

He nodded and in a moment, fell to snoring.

Sayda lay in the dark, dreaming of home. She imagined being out on the terrace overlooking the narrow street, bits of conversation drifting from the open doors and windows. From a rooftop bar came the sound of maracas. What would it be like to be old enough to go there? Pedestrians appeared in silhouette, becoming recognizable as they passed beneath the street light in front of her house. Here came three boys from school, one of whom she had a crush on. As he passed before the house, he looked up, eyes locked on hers. Her heart raced. Did he love her as she loved him? Would he ever talk to her? He passed into shadow and disappeared around the corner.

She awoke from the dream to feel the toe of a boot in her ribs. Angel's silhouette loomed against a pale blue sky.

"Get up. We need to get going."

She clutched her knees to her chest. "I'm freezing."

"You'll warm up as soon as we start walking."

She sat up and rubbed her shoulders, prodded Kelin awake. They ate the other half of their burritos along with a sip of water. They rose to their feet and started walking.

In a short time, the sun cleared the edge of the arroyo and shone straight in their faces. The warmth felt good at first, but soon they started to sweat. Sayda shed her jacket and tied it around her waist. As the heat grew, her vision shrank. She focused only on the yard of sand before her feet. Here and there, the sand was pockmarked with depressions, the hoofprints of javelina or maybe wild burros. These animals needed water, didn't they? Did that mean the river was near?

Hours of walking gave the lie to that hope. The sun seemed to stall straight overhead, cooking her brain. Her throat went dry, her lips parched. She turned to Kelin, noticed the line of dried salt staining the underarms of his shirt.

"Can you get the water bottle out of my pack?" she said.

He frowned. "We shouldn't drink yet. There's hardly any left."

Kelin was right. She had to hold out.

The arroyo twisted back and forth, forcing them to travel two miles for every mile gained toward the river. They could die out here and never be found, their dear mother wondering for the rest of her days what became of her children.

This time, it was Kelin who gave in. "Can we please stop? I need a drink."

Angel found a thin strip of shade against the wall. They slumped down and reached for their water bottles. Sayda took her last sip and closed her eyes. Blessed sleep rushed in. Angel swatted it away.

"No sleeping," he said. "We've got to get to the river today. We have this far to go on the other side."

She pulled herself up and forced her legs to move. She felt like a zombie, barely conscious. Her only thought was about water. To avoid thinking about it, she began to pray. "Hail Mary, full of grace, the Lord is with thee; blessed art thou amongst women, and blessed is the fruit of thy womb, Jesus. Holy Mary, Mother of God, pray for us sinners, now and at the hour of our death. Amen."

She finished the prayer and recited it again. And again. And again.

Jorge started to moan. "Angel, this sand is killing my ankles. We should climb out of this arroyo and walk on the hard ground."

Angel stopped. He leveled his hand over his eyes and stared up at the rim. "You may be right, amigo. This sand is a bitch."

"The coyote said to stay in the arroyo," Sayda said.

"As long as we head north, we'll hit the river," Angel said. "We'll keep the arroyo in sight."

On all fours, Sayda climbed the crumbly sandstone walls. The rock was the color of her mother's apricot marmalade, the thought of which increased her hunger. She gained flat ground on top and stared out an endless sea of cream-colored hills. Where was this fucking river?

On into the afternoon they walked, slogging across side gullies that fed into the arroyo. To avoid the ups and downs, Angel turned further and further west. Soon, the arroyo was out of sight.

Jorge fell behind, the toes of his sandals dragging across the hard caliche soil. Just before sunset, he cried out. Sayda turned to see him collapse on the ground clutching his foot. She called to Angel. "Jorge's hurt."

She turned back and knelt down before him. Blood bubbled from a puncture wound in his big toe. Behind him lay a flat, circular cactus with thick spines splayed out in a star-shaped pattern—a Horse Crippler.

Angel arrived. "What's the matter?"

"He stepped on a cactus."

"Are you fucking blind, pendejo?"

"It's getting too dark to see," Jorge said.

Angel examined his toe. "You'll survive."

"How am I supposed to walk?"

"Cowboy up. You want to die here in the desert?"

Sayda touched his shoulder. "Walk behind me," she said. "I'll keep my eye out for cactus. I'll go slow."

Jorge rose and limped forward. She scanned the ground ahead, motioning him around any dark shape. Then, as if answering her prayers, the moon rose and lit their way.

They had been walking now for more than a day and a half. The coyote said they might reach the river in two days. They had to be getting close. Would the river be wide? Would they have to swim? Rio Bravo, the turbulent river. The pictures she'd seen of it did not look threatening. She pictured a shallow, languid river like the Suchiate, but without all the people crossing back and forth. Surely, they would be all alone in this wasteland.

They crested a rise to see what looked like a long, thin shadow at the base of some distant hills. As they drew closer, the shadow thickened. A gorge.

Sayda ran the last fifty feet, reached the edge and froze. Before her, a sheer cliff dropped hundreds of feet to the river. The cliffs extended upstream and down, as far as the eye could see.

Angel spat. "Chinga mi madre."

"How do we get down?" Sayda said.

"We don't. Not here."

Jorge arrived, looked over the precipice. "What the fuck is this?"

"We got a little off track," Angel said. "We'll head back east until we hit the arroyo."

"You said you would find a quicker way. You lied, Angel." Jorge began to weep. "You lied, Angel. You lied."

"Go fuck yourself, Jorge," Angel said. "Sit down and die for all I care."

Angel started to walk away, Kelin followed. Sayda lingered, glanced at her piteous companion.

"Come on, Jorge, let's go." she said.

He gave her a mournful glance, then pitched himself, screaming, into the void.

***

The rain hit minutes after Jorge's fall. There was no shelter anywhere, not a bush, not a slanted rock. Sayda and Kelin pulled out their plastic ponchos and squatted on the ground. Angel simply stood, rain pouring off his face. After awhile, he sat and pulled himself into a ball.

The lightning terrified Sayda. They were totally exposed on this high ground. Wind whipped her poncho. She pulled the hood tight around her face, but the rain blew in, soaking her shirt.

With just one hand, Kelin could only hold his poncho tight on one side. He tapped her on the shoulder. "I'm really scared," he said. "I think we're going to die."

She glanced over at Angel's dark form. "There's no point just sitting here," she said. "Let's leave."

"You don't want to tell Angel?"

"No."

They slipped away, following the edge of the cliff eastward. It felt good to be walking, to get away from Angel and the memory of Jorge. She no longer cared about the lightning. God would decide if it was her time to go.

Somewhere in the night, the rain stopped. As dawn broke on the horizon, Sayda could see where the cliffs along the river gave way to steep, grassy slopes. Now there was hope. The sun rose. The day began to warm.

Atop a bluff, on the opposite side of the river, Sayda spotted a white truck.

"I see it!" Kelin said. "Is that the border patrol?"

"There's no markings."

"There's a path going up from the river," Kelin said.

"This must be the crossing."

They side-stepped down the steep bank, working their way around the prickly pear. The river below was high and muddy after last night's rain. She reached the bank and stared at the swirling current.

"We're going to have to swim," she said.

Kelin frowned. "I don't know if I can do it."

"Yes, you can. You have to."

She scanned the far bank. "I don't see anyone. Let's go."

She waded into the river. Come on. It's warm."

"You go first."

She flopped into the water and started swimming. The current swept her downstream, but every stroke brought her nearer to the far side. When the bank was a dozen feet away, she dropped her feet and touched bottom.

"Come on!" she yelled to Kelin. "It's not that hard."

Kelin started walking upstream. With only one hand, he must be guessing that the current would sweep him further downstream. He was trying to get a better angle.

Finally, he waded in and started to swim. Right away, she could see he was in trouble. He couldn't hold himself horizontal in the water. Panic rose in his eyes. His stroke became frantic. He wasn't going to make it.

|Twenty-Nine|

Some time in the night, Gallagher awoke to the sound of rain on the truck roof. It was just scattered drops at first, then became a furious downpour. Wind buffeted the truck body, the rain turned to hail. It sounding like marbles were bouncing off the hood.

He worried about the paintjob on his beloved F150. Would he wake to find it covered with dents? And what about those canoeists? Would their tents stand up to this pounding? He pulled his jacket around his ears. Nothing to do but wait.

In the morning, he climbed out and inspected the truck. It didn't look any worse for the wear. He walked to the edge of the bluff. The river was high and muddy, close to flood stage. The canoeists' tents sagged from the weight of last night's rain, but surprisingly enough they were still standing. Someone had placed rocks in the canoes. People were coming out, staring up at the clearing sky.

The guide got out and started cooking breakfast. The smell of bacon drifting up from the campsite got his stomach growling. He went back to the truck for a slug of milk and a Bruce's pecan pie. Sure could use some of that coffee they were brewing. He took a piss, stared at the sky, then wandered back to the bluff. People were lined up to use the shitter they had hidden away from the campsite. He recalled the guide that chewed him out for shitting in the river. Screw them! No way he would crap in a bucket, much less take it with him in a canoe.

The group was packing up, dropping their tents and stuffing them into duffel bags. The guide packed up the stove and put that in a Rubbermaid container. Pretty slick the way he made all his stuff fit.

They loaded up three canoes, but left one empty. Looking through binoculars, he saw that it was missing a center thwart, the hull bent in the middle. Must have had an accident. The guide strode through the campsite to make sure nothing was left behind. Then, he and the fat guy got in the empty canoe. He gave a signal and off they went, riding the fast current around the bend.

Gallagher felt suddenly alone. What was he going to do out here with no one to watch? He could drive into Sanderson for that cup of coffee, but that would be forty hard miles round trip and a quarter tank of gas. He'd seen a road forking off to the east a few miles back. Most likely, it followed the bluffs above the river. He decided to explore that one, maybe spot the canoeing group when they stopped for lunch. He turned the key of his F 150 and started up the road. Last night's rain had turned the surface into a soupy marl. The truck slid from side to side as he drove up the incline. Better be careful or he'd end up in the river.

A few miles along, he came to the side road, just a Jeep track. He turned east and steered around the heads of gullies going down to the river. About four miles along, the track led out to a bluff just like the last one. He parked and walked to the edge. The track wound down through the prickly pear to the river's edge. Over on the Mexican side, there was a wash coming out of the barren hills. A raven glided past and circled to see what he was up to. "Cheers to you, my friend!" He popped open a beer and waited.

Sadness came back to haunt him. What was he doing out in the middle of nowhere? He couldn't keep running away. He had no job prospects, nothing to retire on. He had to do something with his life, make some kind of contribution. Maybe, if he promised to stay in line, the Border Volunteers would let him back in.

Over on the Mexican side of the river, he spotted some movement. He grabbed his binoculars out of the duffel and flattened himself on the ground. A boy and girl were making their way down toward the river. They looked to be alone, no goats or donkeys in their wake. The boy carried a plastic water bottle at his side. He took a slug and dropped it in the dirt. Typical. Gallagher had never known a Mexican that didn't litter.

As the two drew near, Gallagher studied their faces. They were clearly exhausted, their heads slumped forward, their mouths hanging open. Damn! The boy only had one hand, the stump of his right arm covered with a bandage! Must have fallen off a train.

They reached the bank and stopped. The girl studied the river with a furrowed brow. A little higher than you thought, eh, seniorita? I wouldn't try to cross if I was you. She stared up at the hillside where he lay watching. He ducked back, waited a minute. When he looked again, she was knee-deep into the river. She did a belly flop and started swimming.

|Thirty|

After Janey finished up drying the dishes, Ducharme collected himself, returned to the campground, and began to pack up. The routine of packing was somehow sooth-ing—stove and fuel in one container, utensils, pots and pans in another. He and Dagic folded up the tent and stuffed it in the duffel. Others around the campsite were doing the same. This was when he always became nos-talgic, hoping for one more night on the river. He'd be back in a week with another group, but he was going to miss this one.

The storm clouds gone, the sky clear, the day was shaping up to be a hot one. He stuffed a T-shirt in his day-pack, opting to just wear a lifejacket along with his shorts and sandals. "Mr. Macho" Temo used to call him on the Chattooga.

He called everyone together at the river and gave out the boat assignments: Peter with him, Parker with Dagic, Richard with Archie, and Janey back with Lara. He wanted mother and daughter to finish the trip as a team.

"It's 13 miles to the takeout," he said. "We'll stop at Sanderson Canyon to have lunch and scout the rapid."

He got out the topo map and folded it to the last section of river. There were no more compressed parallel lines demarcating steep canyon walls, just squiggles marking the bluffs along the river. He slipped it back in the clear plastic case and snugged the case under the straps of his duffel bag.

"Everybody ready?"

Pooh Bear responded with refreshing humor. "I was born ready."

With just a few strokes, the canoes matched the speed of the swift, muddy current. They whizzed along the low limestone walls, past the clay-colored nests of cliff swallows built beneath the overhangs.

"Boy, this current makes paddling easy," Peter said.

"We may get to Sanderson Creek in a few hours."

As they approached a low spot known as Middle Watering, he caught a glimpse of something odd in mid-river.

"There's something swimming across the river," Peter said. "It's a person!"

"Let's paddle over to him," Ducharme said. "I think he's in trouble."

"Shit, he's only got one hand."

"Don't let him grab the gunwale. He'll tip us over."

As the canoe drew near, the boy looked up with panicked eyes. Ducharme stripped off his life jacket and held it up. "Mira! Tomalo!"

He tossed it in the water. The boy clutched it to his chest. Ducharme unraveled the stern line and trailed it in the water.

"Grab the rope!" he said. "La cuerda!"

The boy swam to it and held on with his one hand.

"There's a girl over on the left bank," Peter said. "They must be together."

"Alright. Let's go."

With the boy trailing behind, they paddled across to the Texas side. As they neared the shore, the girl jumped in the water and helped the boy onto the bank. He slumped on the ground and began to cry.

Ducharme signaled to the other canoes. "Everybody over here! Eddy out next to shore."

Dagic arrived first. "What's the story?"

"This kid was trying to swim across the river. He would've drowned if we hadn't come along. That looks like his sister."

"They must be illegals."

"Probably right. He wasn't swimming for the fun of it. Do any of you speak Spanish? I only know a few words."

"I do," Lara said.

"Ask them where they're trying to go?"

"A donde estas tratando de ir?" Lara said.

"No nos importa," the girl said. "Solo queremos buscar asilo."

"She said it's not important. They just want 'something.' I think she said 'asylum.'"

"Let's give them some water and food," Ducharme said. "God knows how far they've come."

"I've got the lunch stuff," Richard said. He and Archie beached their canoe and started unhooking the straps. Ducharme unclipped his water bottle, climbed out, and offered it to the girl. It was then that he saw a man striding down the bluff.

"We've got company," he said.

Dagic turned around. "Border patrol?"

"I don't think so."

"Good morning, folks," the man said. "Catch yourselves some wets?"

Ducharme sized him up—cowboy hat, white handlebar moustache, pistol around his waist. "Who are you, sir?"

"Texas Border Brigade," the man said. "We assist the U.S. Border Patrol in stopping illegals."

He turned to the two kids. "Can you two show me some identification? Prove that you're U.S. citizens?"

They stood silent.

"You're not the law," Dagic said.

The man rested a hand on his revolver. "I'm the law if I say I am. And who the fuck are you? You don't sound like you're from here."

"The kid was about to drown," Ducharme said. "We just helped him ashore."

"I saw it. But unless they can produce some identification, they have to go back."

Blood rushed to Ducharme's head. "Fuck you, man. We're not going to take them back just because you say so."

"You fucking river guides. You don't give a shit about your country. This is the U.S. of A!" He grabbed the kids by their arms and pulled them towards the river. "Get your heinies back to Mexico! Vamos!"

Dagic turned to Ducharme. "Are you going to let him do this?"

He hesitated. If he physically intervened with this guy, all bets were off. Everything would be at risk.

Lara yelled. "Robbie, do something!"

Fuck it. He grabbed the man by the shoulder and spun him around. The man shoved him back. Ducharme lost his balance, fell backwards. He expected to hit the ground, but landed instead on a bed of nails—the spines of a prickly pear cactus. A scream—high and shrill like a woman's—erupted from his throat. He thought he would pass out from pain. Then, from the corner of his eye, he saw Dagic unsheathe his knife, charge the cowboy and stab him in the belly. Blood welled through the man's shirt, but Dagic wasn't through. He jerked the double-bladed knife side-to-side until a bright pink mass of intestine spilled out.

A collective howl rose up from the group. The Hispanic kids fled up the hill.

Ducharme moaned, "Someone get me off!"

Dagic wiped his knife on his pants and stuck it back in its sheath. He called for Richard, and the two of them each took one of his arms and pulled him upright.

"Take him to my boat," Dagic said. "Easy now."

As he stumbled toward the canoe, he spat at Dagic. "You crazy motherfucker. You fucking killed him."

"Shut up!" Dagic said.

They reached the canoe and laid him face down across a duffel bag. Janey called for the first aid kit.

"Not now," Dagic said. "We need to get away from here. Someone go with Peter. I'll paddle Robbie."

In the midst of his pain, Ducharme was aware that Dagic was taking control of the group. But he was in no position to stop him.

As the canoe reached mid-river, he looked over at the shore. The cowboy was back on his feet, struggling up the hillside with twenty feet of intestine trailing behind.

"Shit, the guy's still alive. We've got to go back, Janko."

"He won't be for long."

He played the stabbing back in his mind. That was not the work of an amateur. "You're ex-military, aren't you?"

"Da."

"Why did you lie?"

"Wasn't your business."

He thought about what lay ahead, when the police found out. "We need to report this. I'll say it was self-defense."

Dagic said nothing. Either he was mulling over the choice or had decided not to report it. Either way, there was no keeping this a secret. If they didn't turn themselves in, both he and Dagic would eventually be arrested. There would be a trial. He would have to cancel his next trip. Once word got out about the incident, he'd be lucky to ever fill another one.

"Are the thorns still in me? It feels like they are."

"Yup. You look like a porcupine. We need to stop and get those out soon."

"We're supposed to meet the shuttle driver at noon."

"Don't worry. He'll wait."

The sound of rushing water rose in the distance. He glanced at the shoreline, recognized the mouth of Sanderson Canyon, below which lay Sanderson Rapid. After all the rain, the waves would be big and the current rushing against the wall.

"Pull over here, Janko. We need to scout this rapid."

Dagic turned around and waved his paddle. "Everyone ashore."

They beached their canoes on the gravel at the mouth of the creek. Dagic helped him out of the boat. Thunder rolled in the distance.

Ducharme shook his head. "Just what we need."

"Somebody put a tent up," Dagic said. "I've got to get these thorns out of Robbie's back and we may be getting another storm."

There was a scramble to find the tent bag and erect the tent on the gravel. Ducharme got to his feet, felt like he was going to vomit.

Janey came up. "Here's the first aid kit. Let me help you."

"No, I've got it," Dagic said. "Get me a sleeping pad."

When the tent was up and the mattress rolled out, Ducharme laid down inside. Dagic entered and zipped the tent flaps closed. He fumbled through the first aid kit.

"Are you looking for the tweezers? They're in the zippered pocket on the right."

"I found them."

He felt Dagic's breath on the back of his neck.

"This is going to hurt," he said. "I can pull the thorns out by hand, but I'll have to use the tweezers on those hairs."

"Glochids."

"Right. Glochids."

Dagic pulled the first thorn out of his neck. He winced in pain.

"So what else did you lie about?" he said. "Are you really Croatian?"

"I'm a Serb."

"Why the secrecy?"

"You remember the war in the 90s? The siege of Sarajevo?"

"Yeah. What were you, a fucking sniper?"

"Da."

Ducharme had read about the role of snipers in that siege, killing innocent civilians, Bosnian mothers and children walking to the store, collecting water at public fountains. It made him sick at the time, but the war was long over.

"Most Americans won't even remember the war," he said.

Dagic snorted. "The lawyers will tell them about people like me, the ones who committed 'crimes against humanity.'"

"You shot civilians. What's new?"

"Not just any civilians, Robbie. We snipers only had so many chances, so many bullets. If I saw a family crossing the street, I would pick out the most beautiful girl. Like our Lara. I would shoot her in the head and watch the blood spurt out like a water fountain. Do you know why I did that?"

"Because you're a sick fuck."

"Because that would cause the family the most pain. And maximum pain eventually leads to surrender. Which they would have done if you Americans hadn't intervened."

Dagic started pulling thorns from his butt. Thunder rumbled again in the distance.

"Put your hands behind your back," Dagic said.

He did as he was told. Maybe Dagic needed to reach some difficult spot. Suddenly, he felt his wrists being bound with rope.

"What the fuck are you doing?"

He tried to roll over, but Dagic pinned him with his knee.

"I'm not turning myself in," Dagic said. "And you are not going to turn me in. I'm in this country illegally, just like your Hispanic friends. I had to flee my country and I am not going back. And I am not going to stand trial and risk going to prison."

Now, it was all coming clear. Dagic was going to leave them and take the van.

He unsheathed his knife and held it to Ducharme's throat. "Now, I'm going to go and you're going to stay. I don't want to hurt you, but I will if I have to. All I want is a head start."

Dagic fled the tent, zipping the flap closed behind him. Ducharme could hear the others asking him questions. Was Robbie alright? What should they do next?

"Pull the boats onshore and turn them over," Dagic said. "We're going to be camping here."

He heard the rattling of the canoes over the rocks and the hollow thump as they were turned over. Then came a strange popping sound. People yelled, "What are you doing? Stop!" Someone unzipped the fly—Richard.

"Janko's trashing the canoes!"

"Untie me. Quick."

He popped out of the tent. Dagic had already stabbed holes in two canoes and was working on the third. The fourth, the one he would no doubt use to escape, was sitting upright on the shore. Ducharme sprinted across the rocks, pushed the canoe in the water, and jumped in. He grabbed the paddle and managed to take two strokes before the boat jerked to a halt. He spun around and saw Dagic holding the stern. This time there was no hesitation. He rammed the paddle into the Serb's throat. Dagic fell backwards, clutching his neck. Ducharme paddled into deep water, safe for the moment. Then, he realized his mistake. Dagic got to his feet, grabbed Janey from behind, and held his knife to her neck.

"One more stroke and I'll slit your whore's throat!" he yelled.

Lara screamed. The others stared, dumbfounded.

"That's right," Dagic said. "While you all were asleep last night, your leader and the lovely Janey here were fucking their brains out. Now, I suggest you get back here, Mr. Ducharme."

Knowing full well that Dagic would probably kill him as soon as he stepped on shore, he willed his arms to move. He beached the canoe and stepped out.

"Turn her loose," he said.

Dagic pushed Janey away and strode toward him. In one swift move, the Serb kneed him in the groin, spun him around and slashed the back of his leg. He felt the muscle pop and fell howling to the ground.

"I'm sorry, my friend," Dagic said. "I can't have you coming after me."

Dagic trotted to the undamaged canoe.

"Goodbye, everyone," he said. "Sorry to spoil the trip."

Sprawled in the dirt, Ducharme watched as Dagic paddled to midstream, glanced back, and disappeared around the bend.

Janey ran to him. "God, what did he do?"

He rolled over on his stomach, grabbed the back of his leg. "Fucking hamstrung me."

"You're bleeding like crazy. Someone get the first aid kit. It's in the tent."

Richard's face appeared in front of his. "What the fuck is going on, Robbie? Why did he do this to you?"

"Janko's a war criminal. He's on the run."

"What war?"

"Serbo-Croatian. He's a Serb sniper."

Parker came back with the first aid kit. Janey got out a roll of gauze and began wrapping his leg.

"This looks bad, but I don't know what else I can do," she said. "You can't walk."

"Someone's gotta go for help," he said.

The men started talking, confused, afraid.

"These canoes are shot," Peter said. "What do we do?"

"Help me up."

Richard got beneath Ducharme's shoulder and helped him stand. He put his weight on his injured leg, cried out in pain. "Get my map. It's in the canoe."

Archie retrieved the map, unfolded it and held it in front of him.

"We're here at the mouth of Sanderson Creek," he said. "It runs all the way to the town of Sanderson. Right there. It's about 35 miles. That's where you can find help."

"How long would it take us to get there?" Richard said.

Ducharme peered up the narrow, steep-walled canyon, pockmarked with pools of standing water.

"I don't know. Twelve hours."

"That means whoever goes will be hiking at least six hours in the dark," Archie said.

"I'll go," Lara said.

"No," Janey said. "It's too risky."

Ducharme agreed. "I've heard there are some tall ledges in the streambed. Two people should go so they can help each other up."

Parker shook her head. "You don't want *me* trying to hike 35 miles."

Richard, Archie, and Peter conferred. They looked at the canyon, and back at the map.

"The three of us will go," Archie said.

"That sounds good," Ducharme said. "Take your water bottles. When you get to Sanderson, tell the police where we are. And tell them Dagic has my van."

The men nodded. Parker wished them good luck.

"Yeah, you guys, please hurry!" Janey said.

As they disappeared up the creekbed, Janey took his arm.

"Let's get you back to your tent," she said. "I'll work on those glochids."

Parker said something about putting up her tent to get away from the heat. "Fine," Janey said. "Lara, help her."

Inside, he lay on his stomach with his arms crossed under his head. Janey took out the tweezers and began pulling out the tiny hairs.

"Am I hurting you?" she said.

"No. Yes." He took a deep breath. "I really screwed up this time."

"With Janko?"

"With him. With you."

Her voice trembled with emotion. "You saved my life, Robbie. You saved my fucking life."

He rolled onto his side. They kissed, the pain in his body lifting away.

"I love you, Janey."

"I love you, too, Robbie."

The walls of the tent flashed bright. Thunder rolled. A storm was coming from the north.

"We need to get out of this streambed," he said. "There could be a flash flood."

"Not before I get these hairs out. Pull your shorts down."

He lay back down, fumbled with his shorts. "I heard what Dagic said to you guys. I'm so sorry. Especially for Lara."

"We sinned, didn't we?"

"We did." He took a deep breath. "Janey, what would you think about my coming back with you to Atlanta?"

"What about your business?"

He snorted. "My business is fucked. My boats are gone. My van is probably gone. My reputation surely will be."

Janey pulled out the last of the thorns. "Robbie, I'm 45 years old. I've just gotten out of a terrible relationship, and I have two daughters who need my attention."

"I won't get in the way."

Lightning flashed, the thunder closer this time. Lara called from somewhere above. "Mom, get out of the tent! There's water coming down the creek."

He rolled over and pulled up his shorts. "Shit. Help me out."

They struggled out of the tent to find rivulets of brown spreading across the sand. He saw a second tent yards away.

"Parker, get out," he yelled. "We've got water coming."

He hopped on one foot, toward the bank, Janey holding him up.

"Hurry, Mom, it's coming!"

The water swirled around their ankles, their shins. He pushed Janey forward.

"Get up the bank. Now!"

He saw the wave coming, a chocolate curler rolling down the streambed. There was a boulder in front of him, big enough to withstand the surge. He dropped onto his stomach, grabbed it with both hands. The water surged around his shoulders, stripped away his shorts and sandals. He took a breath, held his head underwater and popped up again. Something was rolling towards him—a body. It hit the rock Ducharme was holding onto and rolled upright—Pooh Bear, his mouth agape, his eyes wide open. The force of his body against Ducharme's was too great. He let go.

|Thirty-One|

As Lara crouched against the slope above Sanderson Canyon, the storm hit with full fury. Lightning and thunder exploded overhead, the rain came down in sheets. She watched as a wall of water rolled the bodies of Richard, Archie, and Pooh Bear before it, swept Parker away as she emerged from her tent. Her mother reached the bank, then waded back to help Robbie. Then, the rain turned to hail, pummeling her face and arms, forcing her up the hillside to the shelter of an overhanging rock. Her last image was of her mother and Robbie rolling over and over toward the Rio Grande, until the hail blotted out her view.

She pulled herself into a ball and sobbed. She called out for her mother and father, but no one could help her. She was a worthless child, a selfish idiot. Why was she the one to survive?

Then, it all stopped—the thunder, the hail, the rain. She raised her head to see Sanderson Creek dwindling from a raging torrent to a thin liquid sheet. The sun came out, illuminating the muddy tongue of creek water sweeping into the Rio Grande.

She stood, searching the river for signs of life, then sidestepped down the bank. Following the roar of water, she stumbled around the bend to the head of a long rapid. Big clay-colored waves leapt for a hundred yards, below which the river turned and slammed against a steep bank. There, where the current dwindled, was a pale white ball, a human, two humans, crumpled on the shore.

She shouted above the roar of falling water. "Hey, it's me! Lara!"

She climbed the bank above the rapid and, dodging the cactus, half ran down the muddy slope. She called again, and one of the figures raised its head—her mother. She slid down the bank and across the grassy bench. The second figure raised its head and she could see that this was Robbie. Even at close range, they appeared as a single organism.

She dropped to her knees and hugged her mother.

"Don't touch! Don't touch!"

She pulled her hands away. "Are you hurt? Oh, my God!"

There were bruises all over her mother's naked torso. Robbie's, too. Their hips were scraped raw of flesh. Neither was able to move.

"I thought you guys had drowned. I saw the others getting rolled in front of that wave—Richard and Archie and Pooh Bear. Did you see them?"

Robbie nodded. "What about Parker?"

"No, she couldn't get out of the tent. The water just washed the whole thing away."

He began to moan. "Fuck. Fuck, fuck, fuck."

Lara fluttered her hands. "What should I do? I need to do something. Can either of you walk?"

"No, I think my ribs are broken," Janey said. "Maybe my hip."

"You've got to get help," Robbie said.

She stared downriver. "How far is it to the takeout?"

"Five miles. More by land."

"I can do that," Lara said. "I can swim."

Janey shook her head. "It's already getting dark. You could drown in the rapids."

"There's no more rapids," Robbie said. "It's all flat water."

"I swam five miles every day in practice," Lara said. "With this current, I can do it in an hour."

"Then you've got to walk thirty miles," Robbie said.

"I can do it."

"O.K., Lara," Janey said. "You'd better come back."

"I will, Mom."

Robbie told her to look for a white river level gauge that stood against the cliff just before the takeout. "There's a concrete ramp that leads up to the gravel road. I don't think the shuttle driver will still be there, but if he is, tell him to drive you to the police station in Sanderson. Tell them we're at the mouth of Sanderson Creek. If you have to walk, which you probably will, take a long drink from the river before you start. It'll make you sick, but not for another few days."

Lara stood. "Don't you guys die."

With that, she waded into the river. The water was bathtub warm, the current a hand at her back. She started swimming breaststroke, but pushed by the desire to get downstream, broke into freestyle. She could stop if she had to, head to shore to catch her breath, but she didn't need to. This was easy.

In less than an hour, she reached the takeout. The moon was up, illuminating the white gauge by the cliff.

There was no van, but that was to be expected. She touched bottom, felt the rough concrete surface of the ramp. Before she left the river, she remembered to stop and drink. It tasted like mud, but she drank anyway.

At the top of the ramp, she found a body, blood pooling from a wound in its neck. She fought off the urge to vomit. Could this be Janko? No, the dark-skinned face belonged to someone else, the shuttle driver. She pushed on to the crest of a hill. Before her lay an ocean of low, white hills bisected by a thin gravel road. There were no lights, no trees, no telephone poles. There was no one to tell her what to do. No one to blame. The moon was bright and her mind was clear. She started walking.

In the distance, she detected movement. She stopped and stared. Two people were crossing the hills, thin figures with heads hung low. One collapsed on the ground, helped to his feet by the other, a girl. Who would be out here, wandering in the desert at this time of night? There was only one possibility. She hurried her steps. In time, she would be within shouting distance. She would steer them to the road and they would walk to Sanderson together.

ACKNOWLEDGMENTS

Special thanks to Thomas Jones, Burt Kornegay, Jack Adler, and Kyle McCord for their excellent editorial assistance. Thanks also to rafting guide Erin Limkemann for her advice on constructing the accident on the Chattooga River; Ted Thayer of Marathon, TX, for showing me around his train depot; and Keny Murillo for sharing his story about swimming across the Rio Grande.

ABOUT ATMOSPHERE PRESS

Atmosphere Press is an independent, full-service publisher for excellent books in all genres and for all audiences. Learn more about what we do at atmospherepress.com.

We encourage you to check out some of Atmosphere's latest releases, which are available at Amazon.com and via order from your local bookstore:

Tree One, a novel by Fred Caron
Connie Undone, a novel by Kristine Brown
A Cage Called Freedom, a novel by Paul P.S. Berg
Shining in Infinity, a novel by Charles McIntyre
Buildings Without Murders, a novel by Dan Gutstein
Katastrophe: The Dramatic Actions of Kat Morgan,
    a young adult novel by Sylvia M. DeSantis
SEED: A Jack and Lake Creek Book, a novel by Chris S.
    McGee
The Testament, a novel by S. Lee Glick
Mondegreen Monk, a novel by Jonathan Kumar
Last Dance, short stories by Nicole Zelniker
The Fleeing Company, a novel by Kyle McCurry
Willie Knows Who Done It, fiction and poetry by Hans
    Krichels
Witches & Vampires, a novel by Brianna Witte
On a Lark, a novel by Sandra Fox Murphy
Ivory Tower, a novel by Grant Matthew Jenkins
Tailgater, short stories by Graham Guest

ABOUT THE AUTHOR

John Manuel grew up in Gates Mills, Ohio, and graduated from Yale University and the University of North Carolina at Chapel Hill. He now lives in Durham, NC, with his wife, Cathy. John has published three books, including a guidebook, *The Natural Traveler Along North Carolina's Coast* (John Blair); a memoir, *The Canoeist* (Red Lodge Press) and a novel, *Hope Valley* (Red Lodge Press). His short stories have appeared in the *New Southerner* and *Savannah Quarterly*.

John's feature articles have appeared in institutional magazines such as The National Institute of Environmental Health Science's *Environmental Health Perspectives*, and popular magazines such as *Canoe and Kayak*, *Audubon* and *Orion*. For a fuller picture of John's writing, see www.jsmanuel.com.